OMINOUS BREEZE

A NAUTICAL NOVEL

BY
ED ROBINSON

To the people I've met along the way; those that add color to the canvas of life - Thank you.

One

Beth's leg was back on the dock. The rest of her was safely in my dinghy, but her leg was not. I had to go back for it. I didn't want to go back for it. Plan A had been to snatch her up and make my escape before the bums knew what hit them. I had no plan B.

This is how it always started. I could mind my business for months, but sooner or later, someone asked for a favor. The favor inevitably turned into a situation. This particular situation called for rescuing One-Legged Beth from drug abuse, and drug-addled abusers.

Just a few days earlier, I'd been enjoying my solitude aboard my boat. I'd been hanging out in Pelican Bay, nursing my wounds for months. I'd gone up to Punta Gorda to get the boat's name replaced. She was *Leap of*

Faith again, but not all was right with my world. Holly was gone. She'd had enough of my antics and left me to pursue her own dreams. I couldn't blame her. I wished her well, but I missed her.

I was cleaning a nice mangrove snapper one afternoon, when Robin sailed into the bay. I knew something was up the minute I recognized him. He didn't leave Fort Myers Beach without a good reason. I'd asked him and Diver Dan for favors more than once. Now he'd come to ask me for help.

"It's Beth," he said. "She's been smoking crack with those fools behind the grocery store. She's got it bad, Breeze."

"You can't help her?" I asked.

"I'm done helping her," he answered. "She's off the deep end. Stealing and whoring for dope."

"What do you want me to do?"

"I don't know," he said. "You're the smart one. She trusts you. You're probably the only one who has a chance to talk some sense into her."

"You talking about those toothless assholes behind Topp's?" I asked. "Where did they ever get the money for crack?"

"It all started when Beth finally got approved for disability," he said. "They had to give her a bunch of back pay. She was loaded. She went to them for a connection. They all had a big party back there in the mangroves."

"She blew all her money," I said.

"Now she's blowing bums for a quick fix," he said. "It's disgusting. You've got to help."

I couldn't say no. Beth had always been a mess, but I had a soft spot for her. Somewhere deep inside her troubled soul was a good person. I agreed to help. I made the boat ready and took off for Fort Myers Beach the next day.

I hadn't stopped in to see my old friends in a long time. Everything looked the same as I passed under the bridge, except for a few new boats that hadn't been there before. One of them stood out. It was a very new looking Ranger Tug, about twenty-nine feet long. Fort Myers Beach didn't see many brand new boats. The neighborhood was a mix of seasoned cruising boats, and rundown derelicts that would never move again. One-Legged Beth and Diver Dan lived on non-moving boats. Robin's sailboat was obviously able to get underway, but he was fixing up an old houseboat that could not. The new tug was named *Salty Hobo*. Its captain had chosen to anchor in the back water instead of taking a mooring ball. It seemed out of place.

I took a ball. I wanted to take advantage of the great showers one could get with the mooring fee. Money wasn't an issue. I was running out of places to hide my cash. I still lived like the poor bastard I had once been, but it was nice to not have to worry about where my next meal was coming from. I got cleaned up and climbed the stairs to the Upper Deck for a beer. Jennifer was behind the bar. She looked great. She was thinner, and she'd done something to her hair since I'd last seen her. We'd flirted a bunch of times but nothing had ever come from it. It was my fault. Every time I promised to take her out, something would come up. It usually involved another woman.

"If it isn't the long lost sailor," said Jennifer. "Here to tell us some stories of adventure in far off lands."

"I'd be happy to tell you some stories," I said. "Over a quiet dinner some place."

"Same old song and dance," she said. "I've got a man, thank you very much."

"I thought you'd wait forever," I said, laughing.

"You've been gone forever," she said. "A girl's got to do what a girl's got to do."

"Who's the lucky fellow?" I asked.

She pointed at a younger man sitting at the corner of the bar. He looked to be about forty. He was nicely groomed and wore clean clothes, which is more than most of the clientele could say for themselves.

"Meet Bobby," she said. "Bobby Beard. He lives on his boat here in the harbor."

"Let me guess," I said. "Ranger Tug. Fairly new."

"That's right," he said. "How'd you know that?"

"It's kind of his thing," said Jennifer. "He is obsessively aware of his surroundings."

"Jennifer has told me a lot about you," he said. "Nice to meet you, finally."

Jennifer blushed. I'd been a topic of conversation with her new boyfriend. I was flattered, somewhat. I was also a bit disappointed. She really did look beautiful. I hadn't thought about her much over the months. Now she was right in front of me, and taken. Bobby Beard was much younger than I. He was even a bit younger than Jennifer. I wondered about him. Where did he get money? What brought him to Fort Myers Beach? Would he be good for Jennifer? I tried to size him up. He bought me a beer. Jennifer went off to serve other customers.

"Jennifer isn't the only one who talks about you," said Bobby.

"That so?" I asked.

"The gang in the back; Dan, Robin and Beth, they've told me some stories," he said.

"I understand Beth is in a bit of trouble," I said.

"That's an understatement," he said. "She looks like death. I don't expect she'll live much longer if she keeps it up."

"It's that bad?"

"Someone needs to do something," he said.

"That's why I'm here," I told him. "Robin asked me to intervene."

"What are you going to do?" he asked.

"Take her out of here for a while," I said. "Sober her up."

"Just like that?"

"Unless you've got a better idea," I said.

"I guess we just needed someone to take charge," he said. "You seem to be a man of action."

"Just trying to help," I said.

"You're a legend in these parts," he said. "But you're also a ghost."

"I'm just a man," I said.

"No. You go out and experience the world," he said. "No one knows where you are or what you're up to, then one day you show up out of the blue and everyone falls all over you. Jennifer included."

"Don't get jealous," I said. "I've had my chances with her. For some reason it just never came together for us."

"I'm not sure I can live up to the legacy of Breeze," he said.

"You don't need to," I said. "You've just got to be Bobby Beard."

"I know," he said. "But my history is an empty one. I haven't done ten percent of the things you've done."

"Go live alone for a couple years," I suggested. "Try growing dope just so you can buy some food. Eat out of cans for a while. Then come back and tell me if you still want to be me."

"That's not the kind of story everyone's been telling me about you," he said. "They make you out to be some kind of hero."

"Look, Bobby," I said. "You're younger than me, better looking. You must have some money saved up. Nice boat and all. You'll be fine just being yourself."

"I left it all behind to live on that boat," he began. "Now I just sit around this bar, drinking beer. I wouldn't know adventure if it bit me in the ass."

"Then get out of here and travel around," I suggested. "Go see the world."

"Jennifer is here," he said.

"Well there you have it," I said. "I've left more than one woman behind to live like I do."

Bobby Beard contemplated what I had said. I could see him struggling with the idea of leaving Jennifer. He was weighing the possibilities that waited for him out there in the world, against the chance to love and be loved by a woman like her. From what I could tell, she'd be worth settling down for. She had an easy way about her. Her smile was a genuine one. She had long blonde hair with a strawberry tint, sparkling eyes, and a nice body. I figured she was about forty-five, but could easily pass for thirty-five. On the other hand, she was working at a bar in mid-life. She was still a beach girl. The road to success had branched off and left her behind somewhere along the way. I didn't know if that was by choice or not.

Jennifer came back with two more beers.

"You boys playing nice?" she asked.

"Breeze was just honoring me with some of his wisdom," said Bobby.

"Don't listen to a word he says," Jennifer said. "You'll be shipwrecked in the Caribbean with no cell phone before you know it."

"Or in a Cuban jail," I said. "Trading favors with a drug lord to win your release."

"Good God," said Jennifer.

"True story," I said.

"I know," she said. "You'll be happy to tell me all about it over a quiet dinner someplace."

"Exactly," I said. "You catch on quick."

Her eyes said yes. Her eyes said why couldn't I have shown up before Bobby Beard came into her life. Bobby Beard cleared his throat. Jennifer went to him and put her arms around him.

"Don't worry," she said. "Breeze is full of shit. I've known him for years and he's never taken me to dinner once."

The tension was broken. We all shared a laugh before Jennifer went back to serving her customers.

I asked Bobby some questions about Beth's habits. She had been taking her skiff up the canal to the dock behind Topp's every day around mid-morning. She'd stay up there most of the day, returning to her boat before dark. He offered his help.

"Meet me at the mouth of the canal at ten o'clock," I said.

"Should I bring a weapon or something?" he asked.

"No," I answered. "They're just a couple of bums. We should be able to handle them. We'll just grab Beth and get her out of there."

"Okay," he said. "Ten o'clock."

I left the bar after saying good night to Jennifer.

"It was nice to see you again," she said. "You plan to hang around for a while?"

"If I can get my hands on Beth, I'll probably take off tomorrow."

"Figures," she said.

"I'll be back," I said. "Maybe you'll have had enough of Bobby Beard by then."

"We'll see," she said. "Good luck tomorrow."

I thanked her and climbed back down the stairs. I could feel eyes on me as I walked towards the dinghy dock. I looked back over my shoulder towards the bar. Bobby Beard was watching me leave.

Two

In the morning, I was anxious to get going. I couldn't see Beth's boat from the mooring field. I wouldn't know if she had gone to shore until I got close to the canal. I left a little early but traveled slowly. I maintained my cool. I didn't want to get too worked up. I'd just casually walk up to Beth, pick her up, and leave. It would be simple. I'd have Bobby for back-up if necessary.

I was only a few minutes early, but Bobby hadn't arrived at our meeting place. I drifted, waiting for him to show. I drove around in circles for a while. No sign of Bobby. I considered going back out to his boat but decided against it. He was a big boy. I wasn't about to hold his hand. I drove up the canal without him. Beth's skiff was tied to the mangroves, adjacent to the dock. Three dirty vagrants stood on the grass behind the grocery store. Beth sat on a log next to them. They were all laughing and carrying on.

I tied the dinghy loosely, so I could make a fast exit. As soon as Beth saw me, she got up and came towards me. She called my name. Her speech was slurred. She indeed looked like death. She was a small woman, to begin with, but now she was a mere skeleton. Her skin hung loosely on her bones. Her wrinkles were deep creases. Her hair was thin and oily. Her eyes were glazed and cloudy.

I climbed onto the dock from the dinghy. She stepped onto the dock from land. I thought this would be an easy extraction. She went to hug me and I scooped her up, throwing her over my shoulder. She couldn't have weighed more than eighty pounds. I turned and plopped her unceremoniously into the dinghy. She just gave me a confused look. I bent down to untie the little boat and saw her leg behind me on the dock. The bums saw it too. There was only enough room on the little pier for one person at a time. The biggest of the three made a move towards Beth's leg. I got to it first, but he was almost on me. We faced off. I had the leg, so I used it. Instead of swinging it like a baseball bat, I gave the bum a quick jab in the face with the heel of the leg. He never saw it coming. He went down and rolled over backward. He sat on his ass holding his face in his hands. I gave a menacing poke in the direction of the other two, in case they had any ideas about stopping me. They put their hands up like I was holding a gun.

I tossed the leg to Beth and fired up the dinghy. As we rode back out the canal, I saw the bums getting into one of the skiffs. Beth was reattaching her leg. It wasn't a real prosthetic. It was a mannequin leg that she'd found in a dumpster. She held it on with the knees or elbows cut from thrift store wet suits. I couldn't help myself. I laughed out loud at the absurdity of the situation.

"What the fuck you laughing at?" said Beth. "It's been falling off a lot lately."

"It's because you don't have any meat left on you," I said. "You're nothing but a bag of bones."

"What are you doing grabbing me up like this?" she asked. "What the hell is going on?"

"Tough love, sister," I said. "I'm going to clean you up."

"Who said I wanted to be cleaned up?"

"You've got no choice now," I said. "You're my prisoner."

"Ain't this some shit," she said. "What about my boat?"

"It's not going anywhere," I said. "Your friends will keep an eye on it."

"I've got no friends left," she said. "Fuck 'em all anyways."

"That's not true," I said. "Robin tracked me down to ask for help."

"Robin doesn't speak to me anymore," she said. "Dan neither."

"Maybe because you're an asshole," I offered.

"Fuck you too, Breeze," she said.

As we came out of the canal, I saw Bobby coming towards us. Some help he'd been.

"Sorry, man," he said. "I overslept. Everything okay?"

"They might be following us," I said. "Stay here. If they come out of that canal, stop them."

"How am I supposed to do that?" he asked.

"I don't know," I said. "Just get in their way. Hold them up long enough for us to get away."

"I'll try," he said.

"Just do it, Bobby," I said. "Make yourself useful. We'll be leaving the harbor right away."

"How will I get in touch with you?" he asked.

"You won't," I said. "See you later, Bobby Beard."

I took off towards *Leap of Faith*. I left Bobby to fend for himself. Beth pouted and mumbled. I laughed again. It's not every day you find yourself escaping some bums, in a dinghy, with a one-legged woman. Such was the life of Breeze.

When we got to the big boat, I hefted Beth like a loaf of bread and dropped her down on the settee. She gave me an evil look but didn't resist. I didn't have time to properly stow the dinghy, so I tied it off securely. I'd have to tow it. I started the engine and let it warm up for a few seconds.

"Where are we going?" asked Beth.

"Away from your temptations," I said. "About five hours away. Make yourself comfortable."

I had no idea what happened to someone withdrawing from crack, but I was about to find out. I raised the anchor and looked back down the bay. I had no pursuers. I didn't see Bobby Beard either. Before climbing up to the bridge, I checked on Beth. She was asleep. I motored slowly under the bridge and around Bowditch Point. Recent dredging made this an easier chore than I was used to. Once I cleared the channel markers I turned north and aimed for the lighthouse at Point Ybel on the southern tip of Sanibel Island. Beth slept for the entire trip.

She didn't wake up until after I had safely anchored in Pelican Bay, off the island of Cayo Costa. She was irritable and cranky. I made her a sandwich. She ate half of it. I gave her water and Gatorade. She drank freely. Within one hour she was back asleep. I was relieved. I'd pulled her out of a bad situation, but I wasn't sure how to deal with her afterward. As long as she slept, she was no bother. I had plenty of food and supplies. We could last for a month or more away from civilization, as long as we didn't kill each other.

She woke up again after sunset. She asked who I was talking to. I hadn't been talking to anyone. There was no one else around. She swore she heard voices. Later she asked where the siren was coming from. I heard no siren. I managed to get her to eat a little more before I went to bed. She stayed awake for an hour, before going to bed herself. She woke me in the middle of the night, complaining about people talking.

"Don't you hear that?" she asked.

"There's nothing to hear, Beth," I told her. "You're hallucinating."

"They're talking about me," she said. "I know they are."

It hadn't even been twenty-four hours, but I'd noticed several symptoms. She was sleepy. She was hearing things. She was paranoid. I wondered how long these would last. On the second day, I added nasty disposition to her list of symptoms. She was an ungrateful, irritable, little bitch. She had nothing nice to say about me, my boat, the bay, or the beautiful weather. Everything sucked, especially me. Thankfully, she slept a lot. Whenever she was awake, I'd feed her. I made her stay hydrated. She didn't eat a lot, but she didn't seem to have any problems keeping the food down. This went on for more than a week.

I started noticing some changes after about ten days. She stayed awake longer. She ate more. She had some nervous energy, but not enough to actually get up and do anything about it. One night after two weeks, she came on to me. It was pretty shameless. It was not hard to resist. She had only gained a few pounds. She still looked like hell. She'd been a nasty person the whole time.

"There'll be none of that," I told her. "Don't even think about it."

"But I'm so horny," she pleaded. "It would be good medicine."

"Can't help you there," I said.

"No one will ever know," she said. "We're out here all alone. I'll make you feel good. I promise."

"Just stop, Beth," I said. "It's not happening."

"Well, fuck you then, Breeze," she yelled.

"Go to bed," I told her. "Tomorrow we can go to the beach if you're up to it."

She steadily improved after that. She started eating everything she could get her hands on. She walked on the beach a little each day. She slept less. Her mood occasionally brightened, but never for long. She ate so much, we were running out of food. I didn't want to go to town. I wanted to keep her away from other people until she was much healthier, and much further removed from smoking crack every day. I decided to anchor behind the golf course at Boca Grande. I could stay far from shore, not giving Beth any chance to swim for it.

We moved the boat across the Boca Grande Pass and slightly up the ICW. I dropped anchor outside of the channel, a good mile off shore. I took the dinghy into a lagoon and tied up at the city docks adjacent to the Pink Elephant. I walked the ten blocks into downtown Boca Grande. There was a small, expensive grocery store amongst all the shops. I bought milk, bread, and other essentials. I couldn't buy too much. I had to carry it all back ten blocks. I got enough to last us another week. As soon as the groceries were put away, I pulled anchor. We went back to Pelican Bay.

I loved it there. It was home. I'd used the safety and solitude of its waters to heal myself. Now I hoped to heal Beth. She continued to improve. After a month she was more like her old self. Her eyes had cleared. Her wrinkles were less pronounced, due to putting on weight. She was more active and her brain was sharper. She complained about having nothing to do. She was restless. She complained about being horny, but I wasn't swayed. She complained about not having any booze. I hadn't had a drink since we'd left Fort Myers Beach. I figured that if I was forcing her to be sober, I could stay sober myself. I had a couple cases of beer and a few bottles of rum hidden in the bilge. To be honest, I couldn't wait to get rid of her, so I could have a drink.

In the meantime, healthy living improved my physical condition. I felt strong and quick minded. I started thinking about Holly. I thought about Jennifer too. Neither of them was with me, only Beth. I wasn't once tempted to give in to her. I just wanted her to get healthy and remain drug-free. I wanted her to be the friend that she had once been.

She sat with me one night as the sun went down. We talked for a while.

"How did you lose your leg?" I asked. "You've never told me."

"I like to tell people it was a drunk driving accident," she said.

"Was it?"

"Yes, but the drunk driver was me," she admitted. "I've had a hard time living with that."

"What was life like for you before?" I asked.

"Typical middle-class existence," she said. "My husband had just bought me a brand new SUV. I celebrated by wrapping it around a tree. When the leg came off, I completely lost it. I lost everything else after that."

"That sounds tough," I said.

"I tried to kill myself a couple times," she said. "But I half-assed that too. The depression was so great, so heavy, I just gave up on life."

"I thought you were doing okay in Fort Myers Beach," I said. "You've got your boat. You had Dan and Robin. Why do you want to throw it all away again?"

"I've never forgiven myself," she said. "I still get depressed. I wasn't always like this. You should have seen me before. Before I ruined everything."

"I used to see it in you," I said. "Before you decided to become a crackhead."

"Backhanded compliment if I ever heard one," she said.

"You didn't carry yourself like someone who slept in the mangroves," I said. "I could tell you came from somewhere far different."

"Once upon a time."

"You can get back there," I said. "Stay straight. Get a job. Get a life."

"Odd advice coming from you," she said. "You're about as anti-society as they come."

"That's me," I said. "It doesn't have to be you."

"I just don't know if I can ever go back to the real world," she said. "I've gotten so far removed from it."

"You can't go back to those bums behind the grocery store," I said. "I'll see to it."

"I guess I should thank you," she said.

"Are you over being mad at me?"

"Sorry about the way I acted," she said. "You did what you thought was right."

"Start giving some thought to your future," I suggested. "We'll have to get you away from Fort Myers Beach."

"What about you?" she asked. "How did you get here? What happened to make you run from society?"

At first, I didn't want to talk about it. I'd worked hard to forget, but Beth had been honest with me. I told her the truth.

"My wife died," I began. "Suddenly. I cracked up. All I wanted to do was run away from the pain. I didn't have the money to do that, so I stole it from my employer. It didn't last. I nearly starved to death out here."

"Sounds like you're as broken as me," she said.

"I guess I was," I said. "But I survived. I scraped by until the insurance company paid off. It's been one adventure after another since then. I can't even explain how it all happened. I've been on the wrong side of the law. I've been on the right side of justice, in my own way. The river of life just drags you along sometimes."

"What's next for you?" she asked.

"I really can't say," I said. "Get you squared away first. I'll just see what happens next."

"What happened with Holly?" she asked. "Is she gone forever?"

"I don't know," I said. "I hope not, but it's entirely up to her."

"What is it with you and women?" she asked. "They sure seem to come and go."

"This life doesn't appeal to most women," I said.

"I don't think that's it," she said. "I think you're still messed up, just like me."

"I don't give it much thought these days," I said.

"Maybe you should," she said. "You could be off on some romantic beach with a hot babe, instead of nursing me in this backwater bay."

"I wanted that," I admitted. "I really did. I still do, I guess."

"Make it happen, Breeze," she said. "Before you're too old to enjoy it."

"Takes two to tango," I said. "Holly is down in the Keys doing her own thing. Jennifer is hooked up with Bobby Beard. The rest of them are a thousand miles away, or dead."

"Jennifer?" she asked. "At the Upper Deck? You two have a thing?"

"Not exactly," I said. "We've played a game over the years. All flirt and no action."

"She's looking good lately," she said. "She and Bobby make a cute couple."

"What do you know about him?" I asked. "Is he an okay guy?"

"I guess so," she said. "He's just sort of plain. Good looking enough, but no excitement to him."

"What's your intuition tell you?" I asked.

"He's a clinger," she said. "He needs someone else to lead, tell him what to do."

"Does Jennifer take advantage of that?" I asked.

"Not really," she said. "I think she gets frustrated with him hanging around all the time."

"I had a little talk with him," I said. "He doesn't want to leave because of her."

"Maybe they're a good match," she said. "I'm not one to give relationship advice."

"Me neither," I said.

We sat quietly for ten minutes. The sun sank behind the mangroves and disappeared. I got up to go inside before the mosquitoes got me. Beth grabbed my hand.

"Thanks, Breeze," she said. "Thanks for saving me. I think I'll be okay now."

"You can repay me by staying sober and getting your life straightened out," I said.

"I'll give my best shot," she said. "It's going to be hard to do alone."

"Alone is good sometimes," I told her. "You need to take care of yourself. Don't worry about anyone else for a while. Concentrate on making yourself whole."

She gave that some thought. I wasn't sure what to do with her next. Her boat wouldn't move under its own power, but she needed to relocate. She'd always had Dan and Robin to help her when she needed it. Now that appeared to be over. I decided to stay put for a little longer until I could come up with a plan. Beth looked much better. She got some color back in her skin. She no longer looked like an anorexic. She'd be fine, as long as she didn't start back with the drugs. How long did the cravings last? I didn't know. I hoped that she was out of the woods. I couldn't keep her with me forever.

Three

I was throwing a topwater lure in Manatee Cove one morning, trying to decide what to do about Beth. I tossed it along the mangrove shoreline, popping it back to me. I wasn't concentrating on the lure. I was thinking about where to take her to start a new life. That's when the calm surface of the water exploded. A seventy-pound tarpon inhaled my lure and took off across the cove. He couldn't run far, but he could get me tangled up in the fallen wood or dock pilings. I put some pressure on him, trying to stop his run. This caused him to jump. He rocketed upwards right into some low hanging branches. He thrashed about for a few seconds, suspended above the water. The tarpon managed to wriggle back under the surface, but the line was still tangled in the shrubs. Miraculously, the line didn't break. I maneuvered over to the fish. It was exhausted. Scales floated on the surface above him. Blood trickled from the corner of its mouth.

I reached down and grabbed him before cutting the line. The fish didn't resist. Its energy was spent. It appeared to be in shock. I held onto the fish with one hand, and my outboard motor with the other. I slowly drove him around the cove, running water over his gills in an attempt to revive him. He looked at me with his big glassy eye. I dragged him out of the cove and into the open water of the bay. After twenty minutes, I felt him shake his head. His tail kicked. I slowed and released him. He swam away, heading back towards the cove. The fish would live.

That's when it hit me. The beginning of a plan started to take shape. I saved that fish. I'd saved Beth too. I could help her secure a new future, while at the same time take care of a little curiosity of my own. I'd talk Bobby Beard into escorting Beth and helping her get started on a new life. While he was out of the picture, I'd see what would happen between Jennifer and myself. It was a brilliantly selfish plan. I couldn't wait to execute it.

I went back to the boat to tell Beth to pack her stuff. Her stuff amounted to the clothes she wore when I grabbed her, and whatever I could find that was left behind by other women. Andi had left a few things, and she was as small as Beth. Holly's clothes were too big, but we weren't attending a fashion show.

"Where are we going?" Beth asked.

"To get your boat first," I said. "We'll tow it. I'll get Bobby Beard to help."

"Tow it to where?"

"The city of Fort Myers," I told her. "There's an island up there by the bridges. You can dinghy ashore at the yacht basin. You can use the buses to get around."

"I don't know anybody up there," she complained.

"You'll meet people," I told her. "There's a small group of liveaboards there."

"This is a big change for me," she said. "I'm scared."

"You'll be fine," I said. "It's a chance to have a whole new start."

"I get that," she said. "It's just facing the unknown that worries me."

"There is nothing constant in this life but change," I told her. "Embrace the opportunity."

"Why the big hurry?" she asked.

"Because I just thought of the plan," I said. "Plus, I could really use a beer."

We made our way back to Fort Myers Beach. The water was a nice shade of blue-green. It was clear near the passes, as the incoming tide brought clean Gulf water inside. The closer we got to the Caloosahatchee River, the darker the water became. I wasn't up on the latest news about the Lake Okeechobee discharges, but it was apparent that they had continued. I couldn't stick around in that dirty water. It was just wrong. *Miss Leap* liked the crystal clear waters of the Bahamas. Even the Keys had cleaner water than Southwest Florida. I missed that pretty water. I missed Holly too. Instead of attempting to reunite with her yet again, I was scheming to make my move on Jennifer.

I had second thoughts about that plan as we cruised under the bridge to Estero Island. I'd done a good deed for the sake of Beth, but now there was no reason to hang around Fort

Myers Beach, other than Jennifer. I was at another one of those crossroads in life. I was used to it, but I didn't have a very good track record with them. More often than not, I turned down the wrong road. I really needed some direction in life. When you drift around aimlessly, you tend to end up in bad places. I didn't have time to think it through. I was busy finding and tying up to a mooring ball. I'd just play it by ear and see what happened for the time being.

"You, Miss Beth," I said. "Are still my prisoner. You'll not be going to shore just yet."

"What about my boat?" she asked. "My stuff?"

"We'll get to it," I assured her. "Let me go find Bobby Beard first."

"What makes you think he wants to help me?" she asked.

"I think I can persuade him," I said. "He needs a little mission of his own to make him feel useful."

"You're manipulating him to do what you want," she said. "And that will leave Jennifer alone here."

"I'm helping him find a purpose," I said. "It's an act of charity. And yes, he'll be out of the picture for a while."

"You're a slick bastard," she said.

"It's okay to look out for one's self-interest now and then," I said. "Healthy even."

"You're full of shit," she said.

"You're the second girl to tell me that lately," I said.

"Maybe the shoe fits," she said. "Don't leave me sitting out here forever. Go find Bobby."

I found him at the bar. Jennifer gave me a look I couldn't interpret when I walked in. It was almost like she knew I was up to something before I even got the chance to say hello. I took a quick look around, sizing up the patrons, looking for any potential signs of trouble. It was the normal clientele, mostly boat folks, and locals.

"What's up, Breeze," said Bobby. "How's Beth?"

"She's over a month clean," I reported. "But she still needs some guidance."

"You tired of babysitting her yet?" he asked.

"Yes, I am," I admitted. "That's where you come in."

"Say what?"

"I've got a job for you," I said.

"You want me to babysit Beth?" he asked.

"Somewhat," I said. "I need you to tow her up the river to Fort Myers."

"For what?" he asked.

"There's a group of liveaboards there outside the yacht basin," I said. "They anchor around that island just below the bridge. Take her up there. Get her settled."

"That's it?" he asked.

"Not exactly," I answered. "I want you to take stock of the situation. Meet the neighbors. See that she'll be okay. She's a single woman on a boat. She's vulnerable, especially right now. Help her get established. Keep her safe in the meantime."

"That's a lot to ask," he said.

"It is," I began. "I've been thinking about you, Bobby Beard. You're stagnant here. You ran away to live on a boat, but you just sit here, doing nothing. This is an opportunity to see a little more of life, but it's temporary.

You'll be back here in no time. You'll return with some new experiences."

"I suppose I could give it a few weeks," he said. "You hanging around here?"

"Hell, I don't know," I admitted. "I'll probably take a crack at your girlfriend while you're gone. If she shoots me down, I'll leave town."

"I heard that, Breeze," shouted Jennifer.

"I can't tell if you're serious or not," said Bobby.

"Me neither," I said. "You don't have to go if you don't trust her."

Bobby looked at Jennifer. She looked back at him. I'd put him on the spot. If he stayed, that meant he didn't trust her. I gave myself an imaginary pat on the back for my cleverness. There was clearly some tension between the two of them. Jennifer grabbed two beers out of the cooler and set one in front of each of us.

"Look, you two knuckleheads," she said. "My choices are mine to make and mine alone. Neither of you gets to decide anything for me. I'm standing right here for Christ's sake. I'm not the prize in some pissing match."

She'd managed to bring me back to Earth, but she gained my respect at the same time. Bobby hung his head like a sad puppy. He didn't speak until he finished his beer.

"I'll take her up the river," he announced. "I'll keep an eye on her for a few weeks."

"Great. Thanks," I said. "I really appreciated this. Beth will too, in the long run."

"When do you want to start?" he said. "I'll need some help getting a tow rigged up."

"First thing in the morning," I said. "Beth really needs to get back on her boat. She's got no clothes or other personal stuff."

"Is she really okay?" he asked.

"She was a real bitch at first," I said. "But she really came around nicely. She looks much better. If we can keep her clean she'll be fine."

"Okay, I'll help," he said. "Don't screw me over while I'm away."

"You heard the lady," I said. "Her choices and all that."

"I'm going to say goodbye to you right now," he said. "She'll shoot you down. You'll leave town. Adios, Breeze."

"I'll drop in from time to time," I said. "See you in the morning. Don't be late this time."

Back on *Leap of Faith*, Beth was pacing back and forth on the aft deck. At least she hadn't hitched a ride and escaped.

"You okay?" I asked.

"I'm nervous as hell," she said. "Just trying to burn off some energy."

"Look, you don't have to do this if you don't want to," I said. "I realize that I took you against your will. I know I've been making all the decisions about your life. I meant well, but if you want to stay here, just say so."

"I can't stay here now," she said. "I've made a fool of myself. I've pissed off everyone who might be my friend."

"So, you're ready to start over?" I asked.

"I don't know if I'll ever be ready," she said. "So let's just do it before I change my mind."

"We leave in the morning," I told her. "Bobby Beard will tow you upriver."

"Your plan worked," she said.

"He's going to stay with you," I said. "Help you get established. Keep an eye on you."

"What are you going to do?" she asked.

"You know me," I said. "I probably won't be hanging around here much longer."

"You were born for leaving," she said. "I still can't believe you left that cute blonde that was with you last time."

"She left me," I admitted. "Before that, we left each other. We just can't seem to make it stick."

"I wonder sometimes what it's like out there, living like you do," she said. "It seems exciting, but I bet you get lonely."

"I've learned to live with it," I said. "Every time I get involved with people, things get screwed up. Maybe I'm better off alone."

"Now that's not exactly true," she said. "This deal didn't get screwed up. You done good this time. I'm grateful."

"Thanks," I said. "I had to try. I couldn't let you go out that way."

"You're a good friend when you want to be," she said. "I hope you find the right woman someday soon."

"I hope things work out for you too," I said. "Don't let me down."

"I'm feeling good about it," she said. "Don't worry about me. Go do your thing. Maybe I can keep Bobby Beard occupied for you for a while."

We both busted out laughing. She was almost charming when she was sober. With a little makeup and a nice sundress, she could sweep Bobby off his feet. We went to bed still chuckling over the idea.

In the morning, I took Beth to her boat. It was a mess. I'd brought along some extra lines to fashion a towing bridle. While I worked on the foredeck, Beth went below to make herself presentable. A hatch popped open. The smell of sweat and mildew wafted out. She'd have to make her boat more presentable if she wanted to woo Bobby Beard. He showed up on time. After I shouted some instructions, he positioned the *Salty Hobo* in front of Beth's boat and backed slowly towards us. I slung the tow rope over his transom. He scrambled for it, catching it just before it slid back into the water. He tied it off and ran back to the controls, idling away until the rope grew taut. I pulled up Beth's anchor. Bobby kept a reasonable distance between us as I worked. The anchor chain was thick with barnacles and slime. It was slow going, but I kept at it. Barnacles cut into my hands. The slime was slippery. I'd gain ten feet then lose five. I hadn't considered that she'd been anchored so long that her chain would be this bad. I hated that I'd missed even one little detail of a plan. I hoped I wasn't losing my touch.

Maybe I was losing it. I hadn't considered the bums in the mangroves either. They were coming in three skiffs. I hollered for Bobby, pointing at them. I couldn't stop pulling yet. I was almost there. The tension went out of the tow rope. Bobby had taken his boat out of gear. It was drifting back towards us. He bumped alongside just as the anchor cleared the surface. It was a huge ball of mud and marine life. I tied it off, letting it hang off the bow. The bums hovered too close. Bobby tossed me a pistol and ran back to his helm. He eased into gear and restarted the tow. One of the bums came to my port rail. I gave him no warning. I simply shot a hole in the deck of his little boat.

"The next one's in your chest," I yelled.

The other two made quick U-turns. The one with the hole in his boat desperately tried to plug it. Bobby pulled us away. I kept the gun trained on the bum's skiff until we were too far away to use it effectively. I radioed Bobby.

"Good thinking," I said. "Keep pulling. Don't slow down."

"I had to get back to the helm," he said. "Not sure if I could have used it on them anyway."

"You did fine," I said. "See, you've found some excitement already."

"Not exactly what I was looking for," he said.

"Welcome to my world, Bobby Beard," I said.

Four

As soon as we knew that no one was following, I hopped in my dinghy and made my exit. Bobby and Beth were on their own. I left the gun with Beth. I spent the rest of the day trying to figure out my next step. There was an attractive bartender at the Upper Deck that I wanted to talk to. There was a cute rasta hippie chick somewhere down in the Keys that I found myself missing more and more.

I remembered the beer I had stashed. I dug out a case, but of course, it was hot. I threw eight of them in the fridge for later. I could get a cold beer at the bar. I washed my filthy hands and doctored them up. Most of the wounds were superficial, but I had two deep gashes on my fingers. I rinsed them with peroxide, slathered them with antibiotic cream, and wrapped them in bandages.

Barnacles could cause a nasty infection. I knew from experience.

I threw some extra bandages in my shower bag and headed to town to get a shower. I even shaved for the occasion. I found Jennifer working a light crowd.

"You hear from Bobby?" I asked.

"They made it up there," she said. "He said there was a little excitement before he even left."

"He handled it just fine," I told her.

"You're not giving him lessons on how to be like Breeze, are you?"

"I'm just trying to broaden his horizons," I said.

"Interesting," she said.

"What?"

"You totally rearrange your life to come here and help Beth," she said. "Now it feels like you're mentoring Bobby."

"I like his name," I said. "Bobby Beard. Sounds like a pirate."

"There's more to it than that," she said. "You're never here for more than a few days.

I know you've got your friends down in the back bay, but you never get involved in what's going on here. You're in and you're out."

"To be honest with you," I said. "I've got nothing better to do at the moment."

"There's something else going on with you," she said.

"I'd be happy to discuss it over a quiet dinner somewhere," I said.

"I knew you were going to say that," she said, laughing. "Will you promise to be a gentleman?"

"Of course," I said. "Does that mean yes?"

"Just dinner and conversation," she said. "I'd like to get to know you better, but I am in a relationship."

"We can talk about that too," I said. "You pick the place."

"My place," she said. "You won't get a quiet dinner out on this island. I'm off tomorrow night."

She wrote down her address, took my hand, and put the piece of paper in it.

"What happened to your hands?" she asked.

"The bad guys were no problem," I said. "The barnacles on Beth's anchor chain were a different story."

"That's what gloves are for," she said. "You're slipping."

"I seem to be," I said. "Too many people. Too much society. It fogs my mind."

"Sounds like you won't be sticking around long," she said.

"We'll see," I said. "First, I'll see you tomorrow night."

"Looking forward to it."

By the time I got back to the boat, the beers in the fridge were cold. I dug out a bottle of rum to add a little octane to the evening. I hadn't been good and drunk in over a month. It was time to break that streak. I tried to convince myself that the lack of booze was why I hadn't anticipated the barnacles and the bums. My internal chemistry was off. I considered that it was Jennifer that had me out of whack. I was attracted to her. She was spoken for. I felt that I could win her over, take her away from Bobby. Did I really want to do that? What about Holly? I went back and forth with myself until the booze won out. No decisions were reached.

I prepared myself for the big date by putting on my best shirt. As I buttoned it up, a little angel appeared on my left shoulder. I hadn't heard from him in a long time.

"You should go find Holly," said the angel. "You know it's the right thing to do."

A little devil appeared on my right shoulder.

"You should go after Jennifer," the devil said. "She wants you. You can probably screw her tonight."

They both made sense. There was some sparkle in Jennifer's eye that told me I had a chance. Bobby Beard complicated things, though. On the other hand, I hadn't stopped missing Holly. She wasn't just in my head, she was in my heart. Before I gave myself a big head over deciding between two women, I realized that there was a good chance that neither of them wanted me. I was an old boat bum with little to offer in the conventional sense. I was scarred and broken. Both of them were too young and too pretty, to settle for damaged goods like me.

I left the boat feeling less than confident. On the way to Jennifer's place, I stopped at a bar for a beer. I flirted with a waitress. She flirted back. I still had it. I felt better after that. I left a fat tip and exited the bar ready to conquer the world. My ego had been restored.

Jennifer met me at the door wearing a white lacy tank top, cut-off shorts, and a shell necklace. She was freshly out of the shower. Her golden hair was recently brushed. She smelled like heaven. I got a big smile and a quick hug.

"After all this time, we finally sit down together," she said. "Welcome to my little apartment."

"Nice to be here," I said. "Thanks for having me."

The place was quite small. It was filled with beach stuff mostly. I noticed a "Kiss Me I'm Irish" button and a shamrock necklace on an end table. There were lots of photographs on the walls of people I didn't know. I gathered she was a photographer on the side. She brought me a beer and we sat on the couch.

"I feel like a teenager with you here," she said. "Like I'm doing something naughty."

"You could pass for a teenager," I said. "You look great."

"Thank you, kind sir," she said. "But how old do you think I am?"

I navigated the loaded question carefully, taking ten years off my best guess.

"Can't be over thirty-five," I said.

"I'm forty-five," she said. "Now you."

"I'm fifty-four very hard years old," I told her. "Sometimes I wonder how I ever made it this far."

"You're still a handsome man, Breeze," she said. "I've kind of had a crush on you since you first came into my bar."

"I've been foolish not to take advantage of that," I said. "But shit just kept coming up."

"Other women?" she asked.

"Pretty much," I said. "But not always."

"So you've been all over the world in your boat," she said. "And you've got a woman in every port?"

"Not exactly," I said. "I've seen some things. Had some women. I always end up back here alone."

"How many women?" she asked.

"In my lifetime?" I asked her.

"Is it that many you can't remember?" she said, laughing. "How about since you've known me?"

"Right after I first met you," I began. "I ran into my college sweetheart at the Smoking Oyster Brewery. We ran off to the BVI together on a boat. I was gone for a long time."

"What happened to her?" she asked.

"I couldn't give her what she needed," I said.

"Did she tell you that, or did you come to that conclusion yourself?"

"I hadn't gotten over the death of my wife at the time," I said. "I was incapable."

"Incapable of what?" she asked.

"Of giving all of myself," I admitted. "I really had a tough time dealing with losing my wife."

"Sorry," she said. "What happened after that?"

"We playing twenty questions?" I asked.

"It's just that I don't really know you," she said. "We dance around each other in the bar every six months or so, but we've never sat down and talked like this. It's nice."

"It would take forever to recount the past five years," I said. "So much water under my keel."

"I'm asking about the women," she said. "A man's history with women says a lot about him."

"Let's see, there was Yolanda," I said. "But we never had sex. I smuggled her into the country from Cuba. We were together for months. I liked her. It remained innocent."

"Was she pretty?"

"She was," I said. "And virtuous."

"Surprised you left her with her virtue intact," she chuckled.

"Wasn't easy sometimes," I admitted. "After her, I met Joy, right here in the harbor. She was on a sailboat."

"How'd that go?" she asked.

"She got shot and killed in Miami," I said. "I was with her."

"Shit," she said. "I remember now. Sorry, I forgot about that."

"Moving on," I said. "I had a thing with a lawyer up in Punta Gorda."

"What ended that?" she asked.

"Holly shot her on a beach in the Bahamas," I said.

"Get out!" she said. "That's crazy."

"A bunch of bad shit went down before that happened," I said. "Long story. She turned out to be an evil bitch."

"I bet she was hot," she said. "All the really hot chicks are evil bitches."

"She was so hot she blinded me," I said. "I never saw the evil coming."

"So you've been through four beauties and none of them worked out," she said.

"Five," I said. "Holly makes five."

"The girl with the dreads that you had in the bar last year," she said. "She's a cutie, but way too young for you. I wasn't sure if you two were a couple."

"I've told myself that she's too young for me a hundred times," I said. "She's probably told herself I'm too old for her a hundred times. Still, we had an interesting relationship for quite some time."

"How did you screw that one up?"

"Not that I didn't screw up, but none of these relationships ended in anger," I said. "Ask any of them. They'll tell you what a great guy I am."

"A great guy who can't stay in a relationship," she said. "That will affect your score negatively."

"Say what?"

"Jen's Prospective Partner Quiz," she said. "So far, you're failing the long term relationship section."

"I would have stayed with my wife forever," I said. "She was my world, my universe, and my reason for living. All I ever wanted was for her to be happy. She made me as happy as a man can be. That ought to count for something."

"I'm sorry," she said. "I was just joking. You don't have to talk about it."

"When do I get to ask the questions?" I asked.

"What do you want to know?" she said.

"You're forty-five, very attractive, and still not settled down with a man," I said. "I'm guessing Bobby Beard won't last."

"I'm as bad as you are," she said. "To be honest with you, I'm not good at picking men."

"May I make an observation?" I asked. "Something happened to you since I was here last. You seem happier. You've got a spring in your step. Your hair is different. You're thinner. You seem to be enjoying life. Is it Bobby?"

"God no," she said. "I was happy before he came along."

"So what's the deal?" I asked.

"First I made the stupid decision to move to Colorado to be with a man," she began. "He was an old boyfriend. After a few days, he simply changed his mind. Didn't want me after all."

"Ouch," I said. "What did you do?"

"I came crawling back here with my tail between my legs," she said. "I was so embarrassed, but I got my old job back. I found this place. I have friends here that helped me get through it."

"I don't see how this helped you find happiness," I said.

"Well, it's like this," she said. "I woke up one day and felt really grateful for what I had. My job, my apartment, my friends. I simply accepted where I was in life. I'm just a beach girl at heart. I've got everything I need right here on this island. Life is good."

"It shows in your eyes and in your smile," I told her. "It's a very attractive look on you."

"I really am happy, Breeze," she said. "You should try it."

"You think you'll ever want to leave here?" I asked.

"Never say never," she said. "But I can't see it happening."

"I was considering making a proposal," I said. "But your acceptance doesn't seem likely at this point."

"A proposal?" she said. "Now that is crazy."

"Not that kind of proposal," I said. "An offer."

"Shoot," she said.

"When you get a couple of days off," I started. "Come with me on the boat. We'll go to Pelican Bay. See if you like the boat life. See how we hit it off."

"Like a trial run?" she asked.

"We're both adults," I said. "We don't need to beat around the bush."

"Wow," she said. "I don't know if I can do that."

"Why not?" I asked. "It's just two days. If it doesn't work out, oh well."

"I have Bobby to consider," she said. "And I'm afraid I'd like the boat life. I'm afraid that I'd like you. Next thing you know I'm off to some tropical island, drinking coconut milk and sunbathing nude."

"That's my dream," I said.

"With me?" she asked. "Ridiculous."

"It wasn't specifically with you," I admitted. "I've just had this dream to run away from it all with a beautiful woman. Live in the islands. Reject society. Be free."

"So I'm just your latest attempt," she said. "What am I? Number six?"

"That's not fair," I said. "Admit it. We've got something going on between us."

"I admit it, okay?" she said. "But whatever it is, it's never been consummated. I haven't decided if it ever will."

"Neither have I," I said.

"What's that mean?"

"It means that I haven't decided if I'd have sex with you," I said. "I want to. Part of me hopes, or at least hoped, that it would come to that, but I haven't made up my mind if I'd go through with it."

"You're a strange man, Breeze," she said. "Is this a clever ploy to make me want to jump in the sack with you?"

"I don't know. Is it working?"

We both laughed for several minutes. She got up to check on dinner, still laughing. She came back with a plate of baked fish and crisp green beans. She offered me a glass of wine, but I opted to stick with beer.

"I have to know," she said. "Why in the world would you hesitate to have sex with me, especially after inviting me to go on your boat for a little test drive?"

"Holly," I said. "Sorry, just being honest. We are not together. I wouldn't be cheating on her, but she's still on my mind."

"And I have Bobby," she said. "Bobby Beard, the middle-class pirate with nary a raid to his resume."

"That's funny," I said. "I see him the same way. Run off to find adventure, then hide from it at every turn."

"He's staying here because of me," she said. "It's flattering."

"Are you really into him?" I asked. "Say the word and I'm out of the picture."

"He's nice," she said. "He's intelligent. He's got some money, I assume. He keeps himself clean and reasonably sober. He worships the ground I walk on."

"But?" I said.

"I don't know," she said. "He's just missing something. He's got no spark. He's so vanilla and middle of the road, I can't stand it sometimes. He worked the same job for twenty years. He started his own company then sold it. He'd never been out of his hometown until he came here."

"Sounds like a regular guy to me," I said. "Stable, faithful and whatnot."

"I can't help but compare him to you," she said. "You're bigger than life. You're a legend. You said yourself that it would take forever to recount just the past five years. You live life like no one I've ever known. You're your own man. Nobody tells you what to do or where to go."

"It hasn't been all beaches and sunsets," I said.

"I realize that," she said. "There's rumors about you running drugs, or running from the law."

"Those rumors were once true," I said. "That's all behind me now."

"You were on the TV in the bar," she said. "First as the infamous person of interest. Later as the hero who brought that poor woman's killer to justice. Now you tell me your girlfriend shot your ex-girlfriend. Who lives that kind of life? You've experienced more than ten men. Bobby is just Bobby. Bless his heart."

"It all came with a cost," I told her. "I've not been an angel. I'm trying to do better now. I've saved up enough to be able to help when I can."

"I'm trying to tell you that it gives a girl chills," she said. "Mysterious stranger with a sordid past."

"What are we going to do with each other?" I asked.

"Fuck it," she said.

I gave her a quizzical look. She reached out a hand towards me. I took it. She pulled me up and led me to a cramped but very feminine bedroom. I stood with my back to the bed. She pulled off her top. She turned her back to me.

"Bra clasp," she said.

I dutifully unhooked it.

She turned back to face me. Her shorts hit the floor. She wore sexy little panties that almost weren't there at all. Breeze Junior woke up like someone had rung a bell for one of Pavlov's dogs. The panties landed on top of the shorts. She unbuttoned my best shirt. I tossed it across the room like a dirty old rag. She undid the button on my shorts. I helped her with the zipper and they dropped to my feet.

Very gently, she put her hands on my chest and nudged me backward until I was on the bed. I tossed my boxers in the general direction of my shirt. She climbed on top of me and put one hand over my mouth.

"We can't worry about Holly, or Bobby, or anyone else in the world right now," she said. "You might leave tomorrow, and I can't let you go without this happening between us."

I understood. I did not resist. I couldn't have resisted if I wanted to. I'm glad I didn't.

Sometimes the first time can be awkward. We didn't have that problem. Maybe it was because we each sensed it might be the last time for us, the only time. She was equal parts giver and receiver. She was sometimes caring and sometimes aggressive. She stayed on top, taking care of herself but pleasing me until the shuddering began. I held her hips with both hands and watched her bite her bottom lip. She made soft sounds of pleasure. That's when I reversed our positions. We managed to flip over without becoming separated. Once on top, I gave up resisting. There was no longer a need to hold back. She rocked with me, encouraging me. Her hands were soft but her nails were sharp. It wasn't wild passion. It wasn't calm and careful either. It was a combination of care and lust. I liked it. My respect for her grew.

It ended with two piles of flesh lying next to each other. One was pretty, soft and perfumed. The other was leathery, unshaven, and totally spent.

"You'll not get a round two after that," I said.

"It's okay," she said. "Now I know. I don't have to wonder anymore."

"Wonder what?"

"How it would be with you," she said. "How it would be with us. I won't have to fantasize anymore. Now I know."

"It was all you," I said. "And you are awesome."

"Takes two to tango," she said.

"We did it right then," I said.

"That we did."

We got dressed without speaking. There was no mention of Bobby Beard or Jolly Holly. It was late. I had a long walk back to the dinghy dock.

"What will you do next, Breeze?" she asked. "I know you can't stay here. Wouldn't be you if you did."

"I don't know," I said. "I did my thing for Beth. Before that, I was rather enjoying my downtime in Pelican Bay."

"Can I give you a piece of advice?"

"Sure."

"Go find Holly," she said. "Go down to the Keys and find her and give her what she needs."

"I don't know if I can do that," I said.

"You won't know if you don't try," she said. "But you've really got to try."

"I see how it is," I said. "Use me up and run me out of town."

"Look," she began. "I don't know what's going to happen with Bobby and me, but this is my home. This place has been my happiness. My roots are pretty deep. I want you to be happy too. You've got no roots. Maybe you can put some down with Holly. Maybe you two can live happily ever after on a boat. I don't know, but you'll not find what you're looking for hiding out in Pelican Bay talking to the seagulls."

"Point taken," I said. "I'll think it over."

"Don't think," she said. "Do."

I walked to the door. She came to me. She put her arms around me and gave me a long, deep, meaningful kiss. For a few seconds, we were lovers again. Then she slapped me on the ass and told me to beat it. Out the door I went.

Five

I didn't stop for a beer on the way back. Earlier, I thought I'd end the night with another good drinking session, but I didn't need it. I was satisfied. Jennifer had proven to be a quality person, an excellent lover, and much wiser than I'd given her credit for. It had been a wonderful night. I could sleep, carefree and peacefully.

Except for the fact that two members of the mangrove mob were waiting for me on my boat. Two battered skiffs were tied off. Two dirty vagrants sat in my chairs. I had nothing that I could use as a weapon. I had no phone. I considered knocking on a neighbor's boat. I could ask them to call the police, but the last thing I wanted was to make myself known to law enforcement. I sized up the motley pair. Neither was much of a physical specimen. They were poorly nourished crackheads and nothing more. I'd have to remove them myself.

I hovered just off the stern of *Leap of Faith*.

"What do you want?" I yelled.

"What did you do with Beth?"

"She's moved on," I told them. "Nothing for you to be concerned with."

"You messed up a good thing for us. Plus we'd like to pay you back for busting up our buddy."

"He's the smart one for not coming out here with you," I said. "Leave peacefully and no one gets hurt."

"There's two of us, dumbass."

"Two skinny, dirty ass punks," I said. "I will hurt you if you don't get off my boat."

"We'll see about that."

"Have it your way," I said.

I came up quick on the starboard side. I jumped over the rail. I released one of their skiffs and tied off my dinghy. The skiff took off with the current at a quick pace. I positioned myself on the side walk-around. Only one of them could come at me at a time.

"My boat!" one of them yelled. "I can't lose my boat."

The other one held a short piece of pipe in his right hand. He'd have very little room to swing it in the narrow area where I stood. I watched him take stock of the situation. His friend's boat was quickly escaping. I saw him give in.

"Ah screw it," he said. "Come on. Let's go get your boat."

They got into the remaining skiff and left in the direction of the runaway boat. I quickly slipped inside to grab my shotgun. I brought it out on deck so they could see it. I hoped it would prevent them from coming back.

I took a look around the salon. Nothing was missing that I could see. If the damn fools had been a little smarter, they'd have looked for some of my hidden cash instead of trying to get revenge. I supposed they didn't wind up becoming homeless crack smokers due to their intelligence. They'd even left my rum untouched. They hadn't been much more than an inconvenience, but it was time to put locks on the doors.

I'd walked home in a cloud of contentment. The bums had burst that bubble. Instead of embracing the memory of a pleasant evening, I needed to take stock of my life. I needed to decide what to do next. Jennifer had advised me to go after Holly. The kiss at the door had a finality to it. As good as it had been, she wasn't my future. Fort Myers Beach wasn't my final destination. It was time to move on, whether I searched for Holly or not.

I sat in my deck chair with the shotgun on my lap. What about Beth? What about Bobby Beard? I almost felt bad that Bobby's woman had betrayed him. As far as getting her into bed, my plan had worked perfectly. The fact that it had been her idea lessened my guilt, but I couldn't let him rot away in the barnacle infested waters of Fort Myers Beach if he had no future with Jennifer. I owed him for helping with Beth. I guess I owed him for sleeping with his girlfriend. The only way I could think of to help him was to get him out of there. He'd resist because of Jennifer.

I thought on it for an hour. I decided to enlist Jennifer's opinion. It was time to go, but I could stay one more day in order to talk to her.

My first order of business the next morning was to walk to the hardware store. I purchased padlocks and hasps for each of my boat doors. I installed them without a hitch. Now I'd need to remember to carry the keys with me everywhere I went. I looked at my handiwork. If someone really wanted to get in, and they had some tools, they could. Locks work on honest people. For now, though, it would prevent the bums from just walking in whenever I was away from the boat. It wasn't a bad idea for the Keys either. Key West was notorious for theft. Marathon had gotten worse over the past few years as well. Installing locks was a poor indictment of what society was becoming, even the boating society.

I spent the rest of the day getting water and going to the grocery store. I had to go several miles down the river to get to the Publix. I would not be welcome, ever again, at the Topp's where the bums hung out. I stopped my work in time to get a shower before going to visit Jennifer at the bar. I wanted to get there before it got too busy to carry on a conversation with her. My best shirt was dirty, so I put on my second best shirt and made my way to the Upper Deck.

There were only a few drinkers at the bar. The place would get crowded after the music started. Jennifer was loading beers into a cooler.

"I really didn't expect to see you today," she said.

"Something I wanted to discuss with you before I left," I said.

"You going to the Keys?"

"Not just yet," I said. "I have an idea that needs your approval."

"Nothing you do needs my approval," she said.

"This involves you, and Bobby," I said.

"He called this morning," she said. "Still getting the lay of the land. Everything is okay so far."

"Let me get to the point," I said. "Do you see a future with him? Honestly, is this thing going to last?"

"Probably not," she said. "I woke up with a different perspective this morning. Thanks to you."

"Why did he give up everything and buy a boat in the first place?" I asked.

"Adventure. Freedom," she answered.

"But he's tied down here because of you, right?"

"Yes, exactly," she said. "Am I supposed to feel bad about that? Not everyone is like you, Breeze. Maybe he's happy staying here."

"If you give him his freedom, I'll help him with the adventure," I said.

"What do you mean give him his freedom?" she asked.

"Dump him. Break up with him," I said. "Tell him to beat it."

"Send him on his merry way?" she asked. "He won't take it well."

"He'll get over it," I said. "He can follow me to the Keys. We'll see what we can get into."

"But he's not coming back for a few weeks," she said.

"I'll go hang out in Pelican Bay," I said. "I'll come back in a few weeks. Let him down easy. I'll help him get over you."

"Feeling guilty?" she asked.

"Absolutely not," I said. "Last night was a good thing. I've got no regrets."

"Neither do I," she said, blushing a little. "But you were supposed to ride off into the sunset."

"I will," I said. "I'll just be taking Bobby Beard with me."

"You think you'll be rescuing us both, no doubt," she said.

"If the shoe fits, darling."

"I think it does," she said. "This could be a good thing. You sure have shaken things up this time."

"I just came here to help Beth," I said. "The rest of it just kind of happened."

"You're a man of action," she said. "I'll give you that."

"For the next few weeks, I'll be a man lying on a beach," I said. "My invitation remains open."

"Don't start that again," she said. "I spent all night talking myself out of it."

"Okay, we'll wait for Beth to get settled in," I said. "When Bobby comes back we execute the plan. I'll be out of your hair after that."

"Go drink somewhere else," she said. "I've got customers to take care of."

"No problem," I said. "And thanks."

"Thank you, Breeze."

She was a good one, but I was leaving her behind. I was also taking her boyfriend. It seemed strange, but she thanked me for it. I had a new career breaking up happy couples for my personal gain. Except, if she were completely happy she wouldn't have agreed to it. Bobby's days were numbered. I was just speeding up the process. There was a whole wide world out there for him to explore. There'd be other women.

I walked down to the beach in time to catch the sunset. I went out to the end of the fishing pier and watched it dip into the Gulf. Tourists took pictures. Couples held hands. As soon as it disappeared the crowd turned back towards the beach. Only the fishermen stayed behind. I walked back through Times Square and turned onto Estero Boulevard. I had no destination. Eventually, I wound up back at the dinghy dock. When I got to my boat, no skiffs were tied alongside. No bums sat in my deck chairs. I was relieved. I'd stowed a piece of pipe of my own in the dinghy, but I didn't want to use it.

I left early the next day. Just being underway gave me a sense of freedom. I absolutely loved the stretch of water between Sanibel and Cayo Costa. Dolphins played in my bow wake. Pelicans perched on the channel markers. The further I got from the Caloosahatchee River, the clearer the water became. I entered Pelican Bay, anchored in my usual spot, and just took it all in. This was my happy place. I had a few weeks to decompress. I had a few weeks to figure out how to make things right with Holly, assuming I could find her. I was also assuming that she hadn't found someone else. I was assuming she'd want to see me. I was assuming a lot.

I waited for all the boats to leave from the park service docks. I took a fishing rod over there and jigged the pilings and the floating dock, looking for dinner. I managed to land a small grouper. He was two inches short of legal. I'd broken plenty of laws, in several countries, but somehow, I couldn't bring myself to keep an undersized fish. There was no one around to know, but I let him go. I jigged up two more. Neither was big enough. I moved over to the grass flats and landed a nice, legal, speckled trout. He'd have to do. I fileted him while he was still alive, and slipped

75

the filets into some hot oil. You can't buy fish that fresh in any restaurant in the world.

I ate my fish and drank a cold beer, marveling at my surroundings. This really was a special place. I'd have to leave here to find Holly. Depending on how things played out, I might never get back. I resolved to appreciate every minute. I'd enjoy the hell out of it during the time I had left.

I walked on the beach every day. I worked on my tan. I swam just enough to get a workout. I fished for my dinner most every night. I drank my beer each evening but in moderation. I never missed a sunset. I blew my conch horn each time, even if no one was around to hear it. On the weekends, I joined the party on the sand spit. I'd ogled the bikinis and listened to pop country blaring from boat stereos. Each night's sleep was deep and restful. A few storms rolled through the anchorage, but they made me feel alive. All the boat's systems were in good working order. I was in good shape. I really was enjoying my life, except for one thing. I'd dealt well with being alone for a long time, but my mind continuously returned to Holly. I thought about Jennifer too, but it was clear that I'd have to make great sacrifices to be with her. Those were sacrifices I just couldn't make.

For the first time in years, I could go in any direction I chose. There was no particular mission to fulfill. There was no one else calling the shots. The only thing pulling me to move at all was the thought of reuniting with Holly, and my promise to take Bobby Beard along for the ride. I hoped that he wouldn't be one of those jilted lovers that cried in his beer every night for weeks.

The time flew by. I didn't want to leave. I hung around a few extra days just because I could. Finally, I compelled myself to go. I was curious about Beth, and how Bobby Beard had taken the news from Jennifer. I was well-rested, reasonably fit, and ready for another adventure.

The water quality had improved greatly over the previous few weeks. No rain had fallen. The trip went by quickly. I hadn't even finished tying up to the mooring ball before Bobby was alongside.

"We need to talk," he said.

"I figured," I said. "Come on aboard."

I tried to gauge him by looking at his face and his body language. Was he sad or was he pissed? Turns out it wasn't really either. He was excited about following me to the Keys. He didn't let me slide too easily, though.

"So I'm gone for a few weeks, at your request, and Jennifer breaks it off with me," he said.

"Her decision," I said.

"You can see why I'd be a tad suspicious, can't you?" he asked.

"Sure," I admitted. "But it was either going to work or it wasn't. Didn't matter if I was here or not."

"I'm not so sure about that," he said.

"Why would I break you two up and then leave?" I asked. "Seems like I'd stay around here to be with her like you've been doing."

"Well, that's over now," he said. "Thanks to you somehow."

"Let's just leave it all behind us," I suggested.

"How soon can you be ready to leave?" he asked.

"I need a day to restock," I said. "I can get fuel on the way out."

"I'm ready when you are," he said.

"How's Beth doing?" I asked.

"Still sober," he said. "Made some friends that I approved of. She'll be fine up there."

"Good job, Bobby," I said. "I really do appreciate you stepping up like that."

"Still feels like you played me," he said.

"Maybe so," I said. "But you still want to come with me?"

"I've got no reason to stay," he said.

"Opportunity awaits," I said.

"Like I said, I'm ready."

Six

Bobby Beard went back to the *Salty Hobo* and I went to the bar. It was nearly empty when I walked in. Jennifer gave me a big smile and a beer.

"I'm not sure if I should punch you or give you a hug," she said. "Welcome back."

"Why would you punch me?" I asked.

"Because you manipulated Bobby and me," she answered.

"Okay, why would you hug me?" I asked.

"Because you did me a favor," she said. "More than one to be honest."

"The pleasure was all mine," I said. "I wish you the best."

"Just take Bobby out of here," she said. "Take him far away and get him laid."

"I'll see what I can do," I said.

"How soon will you leave?" she asked.

"Day after tomorrow," I said.

"I'm free tomorrow night," she said. "Want to go bar-hopping?"

"Sure," I said. "Why not?"

"Meet me here at five," she said.

"It's a date," I said.

"No," she said. "No, it's not. We're just going to drink and laugh and make toasts to Breeze and Bobby."

"Fair enough."

Fort Myers Beach is a good town for bar hopping. You can walk from place to place in minutes. Each drinking establishment has a different crowd. People watching is top notch. Some of the music is good and some it is bad, but it didn't matter to us. We spent four hours and a small fortune trying to drink all the beer on the beach. We ended up back at the Upper Deck. We stood at the bottom of the stairs, about to part ways. We looked deeply into each other's eyes. Both of us expressed our gratitude and friendship without saying a word. After a soft hug, she climbed the stairs and I turned away, heading for the dinghy dock. *Goodbye Jennifer.*

After my chores were finished the next day, I held a brief captain's meeting with Bobby Beard. We went over the charts together. I explained where I planned to anchor, and the potential hazards of each leg of the journey. He listened, asked a lot of questions, and generally satisfied me that he was paying attention. He checked the marine forecast on his phone. We were good to go.

"How many miles have you put on that tug of yours?" I asked.

"I bought it down here," he said. "I drove it here, and back and forth to Fort Myers. That's it."

"Not much experience," I said.

"I can learn from the best," he said.

"The big thing is weather," I told him. "Avoid bad weather whenever possible. Hole up if you have to. Keep your vessel in good repair and be ready for anything."

"Got it," he said.

"We need three days to get to Marathon," I said. "But that can turn into a week or more if we have to sit out bad weather."

"I'm not in a hurry," he said.

"I don't expect we'll see any excitement on our way down," I said. "But once we get to the Keys, anything can happen."

"I've never been there," he said.

"Stay alert. Observe everything and everyone," I said. "Look for trouble before it happens."

"Trouble?" he asked. "I thought we were just looking for your girlfriend."

"There may not be any problems," I said. "But be ready just in case. Be ready for anything."

"Hope for the best, prepare for the worst," he said.

"Hope in one hand and shit in the other," I said. "See which one fills up first."

Bobby laughed and called me a cynical son of a bitch. I told him that it had kept me alive so far. If you live enough life you'll see some shit. Best to be ready and able to handle it. We put the charts away and I went back to *Leap of Faith*. I had the keys to the locks in my pocket. There were no bums in sight.

I got a good night's sleep and woke ready for travel. I took a look around the harbor. It was a good place, but it was time to leave. We left Fort Myers Beach behind us and made our way south under sunny skies and light winds. We made it to Marco Island by mid-afternoon. It was an easy trip. As soon as we got settled on our anchors, Bobby came over to *Leap of Faith*.

"I didn't realize we'd be out of sight of land," he said.

I had gone farther offshore than necessary, just to give him the experience.

"Get used to it," I said. "It will happen again tomorrow and in Florida Bay, but only briefly."

"How many miles have you traveled on this boat?" he asked.

"I don't know," I said. "Approaching ten thousand I'd guess."

"You don't keep track?" he asked. "Like in a log or something?"

"I don't need to impress anyone with stuff like that," I said. "The boat doesn't care how far it's been."

"I bet you've seen it all," he said.

"No one ever sees it all," I offered. "But I've seen my share."

"What's the most dangerous thing you've ever done?" he asked.

"I guess dodging automatic weapons fire qualifies," I answered.

"How did that come about?"

"I had a run-in with this mean dude in the drug trade," I began. "I was smuggling a Cuban girl into the country. He tried to rape her. He was big, tough and no stranger to violence. I tricked him into coming up that ladder right there. As soon as I saw his head, I bashed it in with a hammer. He survived. Months later he found me and riddled this boat full of bullets. Somehow, I survived, although my canned goods took a beating."

"Canned goods?" he asked.

"I sort of hunkered down below where all the cans are stored. I had corn and bean juice all over the place."

"How'd you get out of it?" he asked.

"The dumbass ran aground at a high rate of speed," I said. "The cops showed up in force. Before I knew it I was surrounded by the

FWC, Sheriff's Department, and the Coast Guard."

"Good thing the cavalry showed up," he said.

"Except the cavalry focused on my outstanding warrants," I said. "I was arrested for past deeds, plus possession of marijuana. The whole thing was a mess."

"I don't think I'm interested in that sort of adventure," he said.

"Trust me," I told him. "Neither am I."

"There's good stuff too, right?" he asked. "Blue water and pretty beaches? Drink in your hand and a woman by your side?"

"Sure," I said. "I know most of the good spots from here to the Dominican. I've been up and down the islands with several women. Great times. That's what it's all about."

"Why do you come back?" he asked.

"Different reasons," I said. "The woman wanted to come back, or the woman left me. Sometimes I just miss home. One time I bought a fancy new trawler to make the trip. I put *Miss Leap* in a boatyard for a total refit. I had to get back to her."

"What did you do with the new boat?" he asked.

"It took a while, but I sold it," I said. "I was near starving when it finally sold."

"How much?"

"Six hundred grand," I told him. "But I had to go all the way to Luperon to get the money."

"Another story," he said.

"A long one," I told him. "It can wait for another day."

"Tell me about Holly," he said.

"She's a funky, free-spirit with dreadlocks in her blonde hair," I said. "She lives to sail. She's an accomplished diver. She's much too young for me and apparently tired of my shit. She's fearless in everything but relationships."

"Why is she tired of your shit?"

"She came along on the first few adventures willingly," I said. "She started getting wary when one of them went awry. I'd nabbed this dude in a marina in Great Harbor. I was supposed to turn him over to the bad guys. We learned they would kill him, so we helped him escape."

"Sounds like you did the right thing in the end," he said.

"I vowed to stop taking those kinds of missions," I said. "Then I broke that vow. She begrudgingly agreed to go with me. It turned out fine and I thought she was okay."

"But?"

"Our last job together," I said. "I told her it would only take a day or two. Nothing to it. Easy money as a favor for a friend. It took over a month and involved all sorts of hairy situations. Sharks, pirates, a side trip to Costa Rica. We both got a decent payday, but she'd had enough."

"What makes you think she'll take you back now?"

"I don't know that she will," I said. "But she didn't totally break it off. She wanted some time. She wanted to take control of her own life for a change, instead of following my path."

"What will you do if she turns you away?"

"I'll wish her well and go about my business," I said. "What else can I do?"

"I hope it works out for you."

"Thanks," I said. "Now get out of here. Long day tomorrow."

The run from Marco to Little Shark was complicated by a brisk northeast wind. It was indeed a long day. After rounding the Cape Romano Shoals, we had to run southeast. This gave us a beam sea. Bobby's little tug had a lower profile than *Miss Leap*, but it wasn't taking the seas any better. We both suffered through it, rolling side to side. Our progress was slow. It was a little uncomfortable, but not dangerous.

After we got our anchors down in the river, you'd have thought Bobby had been through a hurricane. He whined about how awful the trip had been. I explained that it was fairly normal. The flat calm days were the rare ones. On the plus side, he had managed not to throw up. He just needed a little more salt in his veins.

"How do you do this all of the time?" he asked.

"I'm used to it," I said. "But I'm not always traveling. I sit in Pelican Bay for months sometimes. Hell, recently I sat in a marina for a few months."

"You? In a marina?"

"I got myself wrapped up in a bunch of political bullshit," I said. "I had Holly and another person helping me. We needed internet access. I even rented a car."

"How does someone like you get mixed up in politics?"

"Good question," I said. "My ex-lawyer, who happened to be my ex-lover, was up to no good. I came up with a plan to stop her. One thing led to another. It kind of got out of control."

"I'm sensing a pattern here," he said.

"Story of my life," I said. "It's why Holly left."

"What assurances can you give her that the pattern won't continue?"

"None whatsoever," I admitted.

"That's not much of a plan," he said.

"Plans are overrated," I countered.

"Maybe you should give it some thought," he said. "You might have to make some compromises if you want to be with her."

"Therein lies the problem, my friend," I said. "I seem to be lacking the compromise gene."

"I compromise too much," he said. "Done it all my life. Go along to get along. I finally made a break and ended up compromising my dreams for Jennifer."

"I'd be tempted to do the same if I was in your shoes," I said.

"But you don't," he said. "You leave them behind to go your own way. So far you haven't settled down for any woman."

"I would," I said. "If it was just perfect. The right one, on this boat, anchored near some perfect little island where it's always warm and sunny."

"Keep on dreaming," he said.

"Everyone needs a dream," I said. "What about you? What's your dream?"

"Pretty much the same as yours I guess, but I'm not ready yet," he said. "I need some seasoning. I need more experience."

"We're getting you started on that," I said. "We'll be in the Keys tomorrow."

I gave him the lowdown on crossing Florida Bay. The biggest headache was the sheer amount of lobster traps. There had to a million of them scattered about at random.

Sometimes they got so thick you simply couldn't avoid them. The autopilot was worthless. A keen eye was absolutely necessary. It was only a seven-hour trip, but the constant vigilance required wore you out.

We called it a night before the mosquitoes came out in force. I buttoned up the windows and hatches before settling down with a glass of rum and a good book. It didn't take long before my thoughts distracted me. I ran through the various potential scenarios that might await me in Marathon. Holly might be there. She might not. My pirate foes Rabble and Rogue might be there. If not, their buddies might want to pay me a visit. I was glad for my new locks. Other than that I didn't foresee any additional trouble. If Holly wasn't there, we'd ask around until we got a lead on where she went.

We passed Cape Sable and the southernmost tip of mainland Florida early the next morning. As we entered Florida Bay, I thanked the sea Gods for calm weather. I cursed the lobstermen for their excessive use of gear and haphazard placement. The multi-colored floats were everywhere. We zigged and we zagged. We bobbed and we weaved.

The track left on my GPS looked like something done by a drunken captain. Finally, as we approached the Seven Mile Bridge, the floats cleared out. It was only a short reprieve. The pots resumed after we cleared the bridge, though not as thick. We made the entrance channel to Boot Key Harbor without difficulty. We were in Marathon.

Seven

I kept my eyes open for Holly's boat, but I didn't see *Another Adventure* in the main harbor. I didn't see Rabble's boat either. We called ahead to Marathon City Marina and they assigned us a mooring ball. I took Bobby up to the office to sign in and showed him around. There was a gang of drunks sitting under the tiki. They looked like a rough bunch. Kids were doing school work in the day room. Sails were being sewn in the workshop. Some old timers were tinkering with an outboard motor in the back parking lot. The garden between the office and the showers was alive with herbs, ferns, and even some vegetables. Manatees floated below the water hose, hoping for a few drops to come their way. The bike racks held over a hundred bikes of all shapes, sizes, and condition.

"Interesting place," said Bobby.

"If Holly isn't here, I won't be staying long," I said. "You can stay if you want to."

"I can always come back another time," he said. "Where do we start looking?"

"We take a dinghy ride around the harbor," I said. "Then up the creek if we haven't found her."

"Let's go," he said.

We puttered down to Dockside. No sign of Holly. We went over near the park without any luck. I tuned into Sisters Creek and motored along slowly. There was no sign of *Another Adventure*. I took us back to the dinghy dock. I asked the drunks if they'd seen Holly. She had been there but had been gone for some time. They had no clue where she went. We asked around in the day room. We found some folks who knew her, but they were no help in locating her. They suggested we try Facebook.

The day room had free WiFi. Bobby sat down and started poking at his phone. He spent a few minutes looking for Holly Freeman on Facebook. He was unsuccessful.

"She must be using a different name," he said. "Any clues?"

"I've got no idea," I admitted. "I'm not too tech savvy."

"We need to find someone who's friends with her on Facebook," he said.

I went back to the people who knew her. They weren't Facebook friends with Holly, but they said we could try the Boot Key Harbor Cruisers Group. They were sure that she posted to it sometimes. I told Bobby to find the group. It was a closed group, meaning you had to ask permission to join, then wait for someone to approve you. Bobby sent his request. All we could do was wait.

I decided to spend the time drinking beer at the Lobster House across the street. It was still Happy Hour. We stayed until the beer prices doubled at six. There was still no word from the Boot Key Harbor Facebook page. We gave up for the night and went back to our boats. Holly wasn't here. We had no idea where she was. I wasn't worried, though. This was what I did. I found people. I'd find her.

The next morning I tuned into the Cruiser's Net on VHF channel 68. I listened to the chatter until they got to an appropriate portion of the broadcast for me to break in. I asked for information as to the whereabouts of one Holly Freeman. I was certain that lots of people there knew her. There were some differences of opinion on exactly where she was. She had been on Stock Island but had left recently. No one had heard from her in a while. It was a start.

Bobby and I were eating breakfast at the Stuffed Pig when he got the notification that he'd been accepted into the Boot Key Harbor Cruisers Group. He stopped eating to scroll through the page.

"Here she is," he said, holding the phone so I could see it.

"Yup, that's her," I said.

"She's Jolly Holly Macfuggin," he said.

"Huh?"

"That's her name on Facebook," he explained. "Now I can look her up."

"And then you can see all her stuff?"

"Only if her profile is public," he said. "If it's private, I won't be able to see much."

"Can you send her a friend request or whatever it is?"

"Why would she accept my friend request?" he asked. "She doesn't know me. We have no mutual acquaintances, except you. You're not on Facebook."

"I barely know what it is," I said. "But we used it once to find that Cuban girl's family in Baltimore."

"Okay, I sent her a request," he said. "But who knows if she'll accept or even see it. She could be off somewhere with no internet access."

"Go back to the Boot Key page," I said. "Keep scrolling until you see her post. Maybe we can pick up a clue."

I ate my biscuits and gravy while Bobby fingered his phone. His first hit was a boatyard in Stock Island. Holly had been an employee there. There was a picture of her atop someone's mast. He kept going back and forth, looking for traces of her. Finally, he found something recent. She'd posted pictures of herself and several other young people playing around on a beach. The pictures were from the Marquesas Keys. She had been twenty miles or so west of Key West just a few days ago. We were getting closer.

"What do you want to do?" asked Bobby.

"I think we should split up," I said.

"Why?"

"You go find that boatyard in Stock Island," I instructed. "Ask around. See what you can find out. I'll go out to the Marquesas. Maybe the Dry Tortugas if I have to."

"I'm not real confident going into a strange place by myself," he said. "Do I anchor or get a marina?"

"That's up to you," I said. "Plenty of boats anchor in there. I hear Stock Island Marina is nice."

"You're throwing me out of the nest," he said. "Making me fly on my own."

"Buck up, Bobby Boy," I said. "It'll be good for you."

"Where and when do we meet back up?" he asked.

"Just come back to Marathon when you get finished poking around," I said. "I'll show up sooner or later."

"I can deal with that," he said. "I'll have a chance to look around here."

"There you go," I said. "Gravy duty."

Bobby and the *Salty Hobo* followed me and *Leap of Faith* out of Boot Key Harbor the next morning. We stayed together on the south side of the Keys until we came to the channel that led to Stock Island. I wished him good luck over the radio and reminded him to keep his eyes open and stay alert for any signs of trouble. He said he understood.

I continued west without him, passing Key West in the late afternoon. It became apparent that I probably couldn't make the Marquesas before dark. Navigating in the shallow waters there was a poor proposition without good light. I made it as far as Boca Grande Key. It was a popular anchorage in good weather. Holly could have stopped there on her way back to Stock Island, but I didn't see her boat. I spent a peaceful night alone, looking at the stars. What was Holly up to? The last pictures we saw showed a group of good-looking young guys. Had she hooked up with one of them? I had to stop thinking about it so I wouldn't drive myself nuts. She had every right to have a relationship with whoever she wished. I was not her keeper. She'd made that clear.

Maybe I'd come all this way, dragging Bobby along, for nothing. At least he'd broken free from Fort Myers Beach. Certain places had a way of sucking you in. They call Marathon the Vortex because cruisers show up and never leave. I'd managed to pull Bobby out of his own personal vortex. I'd make a real cruiser out of him yet.

I had a dream that night about doors. I was faced with three of them. There was no background, just three doors suspended in space. I opened the first one. I saw my Laura. She'd been dead for many years now. I thought of her less as time went by, but I'd never completely erased her from my mind. She was a million miles away, but I could see her. Between us was a great nothingness. I couldn't get to her.

I had no choice but to try door number two. Behind it was Joy. She'd died in my arms a few years ago. Her bad decisions and my lapse in situational awareness caused her to take a bullet on the streets of Miami. I'd done my best to push her out of my memory, with some success. She too was a million miles away. There was nothing I could do.

I was afraid to look behind the third door, but I forced myself to open it. I saw nothing. I looked as hard as I could, trying to see who or what was out there in that vast emptiness. I just stood there looking for something that wasn't there. Finally, I gave up and turned away. I closed that door behind me. Who was the third door for?

I woke up in a disturbed state of mind. God, I hoped that third door wasn't for Holly. I'd rather it be for me than her. It was ominous in a strange way. Two dead women from my past, with room for number three, is the way I interpreted it. I went out on deck to clear my head. A freshening breeze rippled the calm waters, an ominous breeze.

I shook it off and drank my coffee. I was only an hour or so from the Marquesas. The islands there were small. The water was shallow. There couldn't be many places for Holly to anchor. Her big boat would be easy to spot. The sky above me was blue, but it turned gray out to the west. I didn't like the feel of the atmosphere. I had no phone or computer to get a weather forecast, so I turned on the VHF and tuned in to the National Weather Service broadcast.

A small craft advisory has been issued for Key West and surrounding waters out to the Dry Tortugas until four o'clock this afternoon. Thunderstorms are likely after one p.m. Heavy rain, gusty winds, and frequent lightning strikes are possible. Mariners are advised to seek shelter.

I was far from decent shelter. Hell, I was very much exposed, with no place to run. I wouldn't be heading west today. I was so close. I remembered a small channel that cut into the interior of Boca Grande Key. There wasn't much room, but if no one else was in there, I could tie up until the storm passed. I pulled up the anchor and slowly made my way inside. I lowered the anchor and backed up towards the mangroves. I used the dinghy to run lines to a few different branches, securing the boat as best I could. Then I waited. I watched the gray get closer and closer. I felt the temperature drop and the wind increase. I went inside to stow or fasten any loose objects. I hoped for a quick end to the approaching mayhem.

The storm was a good one. I estimated the straight line winds at forty knots, with some surprisingly strong gusts nearing sixty. My anchor held. My mangrove lines held. The first big clap of thunder startled me. I swear I heard the sizzle of a lightning bolt as it struck the island. I saw a puff of smoke afterward. It was no more than a hundred yards inland. *Miss Leap* and I hunkered down against the roaring winds and driving rain. It lasted less than an hour. The rain became a drizzle. The wind dropped to twenty knots. The boat was fine. I was fine. I retrieved my lines from the mangroves and let the boat swing on her anchor. I still had plenty of daylight, but there wasn't much point in heading out into the open sea in twenty-knot winds. *Miss Leap* hated that. I wasn't too fond of it either.

If Holly was still in the Marquesas, I'd have to wait another day to find her. If she was still there, she'd just been through a wicked storm. There was even less shelter there than what I had. With her deep draft, she'd be anchored well offshore. I hoped she'd made it through okay. I wasted the rest of the afternoon with my nose in a book. I fought the urge to start drinking beer, until five o'clock. I fought the urge to add a little rum until six o'clock. There is a fine line between pleasantly numb, and just plain wasted. I was an expert at tip-toeing right up to the edge. What I wanted was a deep sleep without dreams. I'd had enough of the dreams after only one.

The morning broke with a dazzling sunrise. Winds were out of the north at five knots. It was a perfect day to run west to the Marquesas. I wanted to get there early enough so that I could run back to cover if another afternoon storm hit. I rushed through my coffee. The old boat purred when I fired the engine. It was almost as if she knew how important the day was. Something big was afoot. *Let's roll.*

We pushed out into the big water to find some fairly decent swells left over from the previous day's storm. They were far apart and not breaking. They gently raised and lowered us as we plowed westward. I could see two sailboat masts just off the southern tip of the biggest island. I used the binoculars to zero in on them. As I got closer, I could see that neither one of them was *Another Adventure.* A huge wave of disappointment rolled over me. She wasn't there.

ED ROBINSON

I decided to make my approach anyway. I slowly poked my way in as close as I dared. I could see activity on the decks of the sailboats as I lowered the anchor. The sailors looked a lot like the young guys in Holly's Facebook post. I put my dinghy in the water and motored over to talk to them.

"Ahoy," I said. "I'm looking for Holly. I'm pretty sure she was just here."

"She was," The nearest guy said. "You just missed her."

"She left today?" I asked.

"Yesterday," he said. "Just before the storm. She figured she could outrun it."

"Sounds like her. She headed back to Stock Island?" I asked.

"You ask a lot of questions," he said.

"Sorry," I said. "The name's Breeze. Holly and I go way back."

"She told us about you," he said. "Some sort of off-grid anti-hero. She thinks highly of you."

"So did she go to Stock Island or not?" I asked.

"That's her base these days," he said. "She's dropping some passengers off in Key West first."

"I appreciate the info," I said. "No offense but I'm going to take off and head that way."

"None taken," he said. "She's worth chasing after."

I was close on her heels. I knew where she stayed. She was only a day ahead of me. Bobby Beard had most likely missed her and was on his way back to Marathon. I stowed the dinghy and made my way back out to sea. I'd be there in less than four hours. The swells were behind me now, but they'd calmed somewhat. They helped my speed, even though they pushed the stern around whenever they hit at an odd angle. It was nothing that the autopilot couldn't handle.

A slight feeling of anxiety crept into my mind. How would Holly react to my arrival? Would she be happy to see me, or was I about to intrude on her space? Was there still a chance for our relationship, or was I just an old creeper who'd tracked her down when she didn't want to be found? I dismissed it all. I wouldn't back out now. I'd found her like I always found my target. It's what I did. She knew that. If she were smart, she'd anticipate it. I decided to act like no time had passed and that our separation was no big deal. I'd take the clues she gave me and go from there.

I'd never actually been to Stock Island. I studied the GPS to figure out where she might be anchored. There was a small channel that ran between the Key West Airport and Cow Key, but I discounted it. The boatyards were on the east side of the island. Her most likely anchorage was between there and Boca Chica Key. She'd be somewhere south of the fixed bridge that was part of Route 1.

I motored on past Key West again and made my way into the Boca Chica Channel. I turned north, stayed between the markers, and slowed down. There were lots of boats anchored. Fortunately, *Another Adventure* was easy to identify. I'd found her. I anchored within two hundred yards, watching for any sign of Holly. I didn't see her, but the dinghy was trailing behind her boat. She was most likely onboard.

For good or for bad, our reunion was about to happen.

Eight

I was approaching Holly's boat in my dinghy when her head popped up out of the companionway. She looked like she'd been sleeping. Her hair was a mess. She rubbed her eyes as she looked around for the source of the noise that was my outboard motor. I clearly saw the look of surprise on her face when she realized who was approaching.

"As I live and breathe," she said. "It's frigging Meade Breeze."

"No frigging in the rigging, fair maiden," I said. "How the hell are you?"

"I'm fine," she said. "I was just asleep. Now I'm surprised. Give me a minute to get my shit together."

"Is this a bad time?" I asked. "I can come back later."

"Don't be silly," she said. "Besides, it happens to be really good timing."

"How so?"

"Come aboard," she said. "I've got a story to tell you."

I found a place to sit in the cockpit amongst several dive tanks and a bunch of SCUBA gear. Holly came back up with her hair brushed and the smell of toothpaste on her breath.

"Welcome to Jolly Holly's Treasure Dives," she said.

"Jolly Holly Macfuggin?" I asked.

"How'd you know about that?"

"I have a friend down here helping me look for you," I began. "Folks in Marathon said you were on Facebook. He used his phone but he couldn't find you. Then we learned about the Boot Key Harbor page. You made a few posts there with your new name."

"Look at you," she said. "Using modern technology and shit. Hell must be freezing over."

"So what's with the Treasure Dives thing?" I asked. "I've had enough of treasure hunting to last me for a while."

"I kind of got the bug," she said. "But I don't have the finances to support the hobby. Now tourists pay me to go hunt for gold."

"Having any luck?" I asked.

"None whatsoever," she said. "A few broken pieces of pottery, assorted junk. Nothing of real value."

"That won't get you any repeat business," I said.

"I seed the wrecks," she said.

"Seed the wrecks?"

"I go down beforehand and drop a handful of coins in the rubble," she said.

"That makes them happy?" I asked.

"They think they found coins," she said. "I spend a few hundred bucks. They pay me two grand for a week. So they didn't find the motherlode. They don't expect too. Everybody goes home happy."

"So you're not really treasure hunting," I said. "You're taking tourists diving."

"I'm doing research at the same time," she said. "I seed the known wrecks, but then we dive some reefs and other anomalies out on the Quicksands.

"West of the Marquesas, where the Atocha was found," I said.

"Exactly," she said. "There's a bunch of potential finds out there to this day. I thought maybe my tourists could help me stumble onto one of them."

"So far no luck, though," I said.

"No luck," she said. "So now I'm coming up with a new plan. That's where you come in."

"You didn't know I was coming," I said. "How could I be part of your plan?"

"Because I devised it the minute I saw you," she said. "I need an experienced captain that I can trust. Can't trust any of these clowns around here, experienced or not. You, Breeze, are exactly what I need right now."

"Not often that I exude serendipity," I said. "But this sounds an awful lot like one of my missions. What have you gotten yourself into?"

Holly looked around like maybe someone could hear us. She motioned me to go below. She closed the hatch behind her and sat down at her chart table. She pointed to a place on the chart. It was Guatemala. She looked up at me expectantly.

"Freaking Guatemala?" I said.

She shushed me.

"Not too long ago it was me saying freaking Costa Rica," she whispered.

"Why?" I asked.

"It's Tommy," she answered.

"Tommy Thompson?"

"Word got out around Key Largo that Tommy had recovered some of his gold. One of the conditions of his parole was that he would never treasure hunt again. The Feds wanted to bring him in. They know that there is still more of his stash someplace."

"So he ran to Guatemala?"

"Just took off," she said. "He was ready to go at any minute. Even left his boat behind."

"I think I know where this is going," I said.

"He wants us to get his boat down there," she said. "He'll pay, and he'll fly you back."

"Fly me back? What about you?"

"I'm taking *Another Adventure* down there too," she said. "I'm thinking I'll stay for a while."

"You're going to work with Tommy down there aren't you?" I said.

"He's already identified a bunch of wrecks off the coast of Central America," she said.

"So he needs his treasure hunting boat," I said. "And he needs a good diver. In Guatemala of all places."

"That's the gist of it, yes," she said.

"And I'm just the hired hand," I said. "Neither of you will need me once I do my part of the job."

"You're pretty resourceful," she said. "I'm sure we could find something for you to do."

"If I wanted to stay in a third world hellhole," I said. "Not to mention what we haven't mentioned yet."

"Which is?"

"Not that I'd ever expect to just waltz back into a relationship with you, but moving to Guatemala is a pretty huge commitment. Meanwhile, you and I have no commitment."

"Yeah, that's a pretty big elephant in the room," she admitted. "I'm not prepared to dig too deep into it right now."

"And there's *Leap of Faith* to consider," I said. "Logistical problems to work out."

"Lord knows you'd never leave her for very long," she said.

"So for now, I just get Tommy's old shrimper down to Guatemala," I said. "After that, we just see what happens."

"That's sort of what I was looking for," she said. "You okay with that?"

"Let me think about it," I said. "I'll need to check out the boat. Plot a course. Look into some details. Where are we going exactly?"

"Rio Dulce," she said.

"I've heard of it," I told her. "Cruising destination. It's got marinas and services and the like."

"I haven't studied it," she said. "That's your area of expertise. I do have the charts for it."

"I'll take those," I said. "I'll need to run up to Key Largo to check out Tommy's boat. Have you thought about how we'll get two boats across an ocean with just the two of us?"

"How far is it?"

"I don't know yet," I said. "But at least three days at sea."

"I'd really want someone to go with me," she said. "What about you?"

"It'd be nice, but I can do it on my own if I have to," I said. "Tommy's boat has autopilot."

"We still need one more person," she said. "Like I told you, I don't trust anyone around here."

"I've got just the solution," I said. "His name is Bobby Beard."

"Is that your friend that's helping you to find me?" she asked.

"He's in Marathon," I said. "I'll swing by and pick him up on my way to Key Largo."

"Can we trust him?" she asked.

"Can we ever really trust anyone?" I said. "He's all I've got. He's not a sailor either. Just teach him to stand watch so you can get some rest."

"If I'm not here when you come back, I'm on another treasure dive trip," she said. "Just sit tight here."

"It's really great to see you, Holly," I said. "I've missed you."

I held out my arms for a hug. She came to me.

"I'm glad you're here," she said. "But let's not get carried away. Keep your mind on the mission."

"Once upon a time, a pretty young girl left me due to my all-consuming missions," I said. "Now she has one of her own."

"I think I understand you better now," she said. "For what it's worth."

"I'll help," I said. "As long as his boat is in good working order. We can worry about the rest later."

"Thanks, Breeze."

"Work on the weather between here and there," I said. "Use Cuba, the Caymans, and Belize. I'll plot a course on Tommy's machine. I'll show you what I come up with when I get back."

"Sounds good," she said.

That was that. There was no joyous reunion sex, not even a kiss. I'd been enlisted into her dream. I'd been hired to carry out a mission that was solely to further her interests, not mine. I had to give her credit. It's exactly what

I'd done to her several times. The shoe was on the other foot. I could follow along and do my job, or be an asshole. I didn't like being an asshole, especially not to Holly. I was going to Guatemala.

First I had to go to Marathon to enlist Bobby. I had to go to Key Largo to pick up Tommy's old shrimper. Either Bobby or I would have to leave our boat at Tommy's dock. The other could stay on a ball in Boot Key Harbor. We'd work that out on the fly, assuming Bobby agreed to join us.

The trip back to Marathon was an easy one. It was almost boring. I'd made it too many times. I decided to anchor just inside the old bridge rather than take a mooring ball. It was free and I didn't plan to stay long. I took a minute to study my surroundings, reminding myself to stay alert. A few of my neighbors were clearly derelicts. I locked up before launching the dinghy. I went to find the *Salty Hobo*. Bobby wasn't aboard, but I climbed on deck anyway. I sat in one of his deck chairs and waited. I checked his door. It was unlocked. I checked out his neighbors. He was in a better part of town than I was. He was surrounded by well-kept cruising boats. Their owners weren't likely to be thieves.

He showed up an hour later.

"That was fast," he said. "Did you find her?"

"I did," I told him. "Caught up to her at Stock Island. You must have just missed her."

"I went there," he said. "I asked around the boatyards. The guys there didn't take too kindly to a stranger asking about Holly. They made it clear I wasn't welcome."

"You have to be subtle in those situations," I explained. "Get someone to become comfortable with you. Go to the bar. Buy a few beers. Casually work up to it."

"I just walked into the office and asked," he admitted. "Guess I didn't think it through."

"If you'd have just been chill, and been able to stick around, you'd have seen her pull in," I said.

"I was in a hurry to make something happen," he said.

"Live and learn," I said. "But it's okay. I found her."

"How did it go?" he asked. "You're back here too quickly."

"I found her. We talked briefly. Now we're going to Guatemala."

"What?" he asked. "Why?"

"We've got a job to do Bobby Beard," I said. "You are part of the crew."

"I don't know man," he said. "What the hell? We just jump off and go to some third world country? Just like that?"

"First we go to Key Largo and get our boat," I told him. "Then I take you to Holly. You'll crew for her."

"She's taking her boat too?"

"That's right," I said. "She's got an opportunity down there. She needs me to take some old shrimp boat down for her. To be honest, I'm probably the perfect person for the job. She's lucky I found her when I did."

"Why a shrimp boat?" he asked.

"It's been converted to hunt for treasure," I said. "We used it recently."

"How do we get back?" he asked.

"Her partner is already there," I said. "He's paying us, and for our return airfare."

"She has a partner?"

"A business partner," I said. "Not a love interest. He's very experienced. He's very smart, and I trust him."

"What about our boats?"

"It's like this," I began. "The shrimper is up a narrow canal on a private dock. One of us will maneuver it out of there. The other will leave his boat there."

"I don't know that I can do that," he said. "This is the biggest boat I've ever operated."

"Then I'll have to do it," I said. "I'll leave my boat here. You take me to the dock. I'll move the shrimper out of the way and you come in behind me. We'll use the dinghy as a shuttle if necessary."

"Where's your boat now?"

"Anchored by the bridge," I said. "But I'll put it on your ball while we're gone. Safer here."

"I only paid for a week," he said.

"Go up and pay for another month," I told him.

"Are you sure about all of this?" he asked. "Guate-damn-mala?"

"We'll get you some sea time," I said. "Holly will teach you how to sail. You can swash the buckles and swab the deck. It's a perfect opportunity for you to earn some bona fides."

"Holy crap," he said. "I'm going to Guatemala. How's that for adventure?"

"Hopefully it will be dull and peaceful," I said. "If we play the weather right, it will just be a long boat ride."

"Let's do it," he said. "I'm in."

"Prepare to leave in the morning," I told him.

"Aye, captain," he replied.

We switched places without too much trouble the next morning. I showed Bobby where to go. We motored up the inside past Islamorada and through Tarpon Basin. When we got near the creek entrance, I had him stop and drift. We put his dinghy in the water. I used it to run on up the creek to Tommy's dock. I left it tied up. Bobby could use it to come back out to me. I climbed onto the old shrimper. It wasn't locked. The keys were in the ignition. The engine turned over and fired up on the first try. I let it idle while I checked the gauges. We'd need fuel. Everything else looked normal. I could get water and groceries in Marathon. I untied the lines, all the while figuring out how I was going to make a U-turn and successfully navigate away from the dock.

I'd watched the shrimpers in Fort Myers Beach do this many times. It involved pulling up and back multiple times, using the prop walk to spin the boat. Those guys were pros. I was not, at least not with a strange boat. I had a good idea how it worked, though, so I threw her in gear and eased off. I put it in reverse and backed towards the dock again. This angled the bow more away from the dock. I repeated the process six or seven times. Finally, I was able to head back out towards the bay, where Bobby Beard waited. He put the *Salty Hobo* in the spot where the shrimper had been. I dropped anchor to wait for him. I wanted to take a look around Tommy's boat. I'd spent some time on it previously, but hadn't thoroughly familiarized myself with it.

I started in the engine room. It was surprisingly clean. I checked the oil and coolant levels. They were fine. The filters looked new. The belts were in good shape. The thru-hulls moved easily and the bilge was dry. It was clear that Tommy had made sure his boat was ready to go. Boats like his carried a lot of fuel. They regularly ran from Fort Myers Beach to

Port Aransas in Texas. I didn't think we'd have to worry about running out of fuel, once we topped off. The hold was empty, so we didn't carry much weight either. It was a solid vessel, despite the layer of rust on the outer hull.

Bobby came aboard and together we inspected the rest of the interior. Tommy hadn't done much to provide any comfort. There was only one small bunk. The galley was minimal. The head was very basic, but at least it had a shower. I wasn't going on a pleasure cruise. It was simply a boat delivery. I could deal with the Spartan conditions for the three or four days it would take to reach my destination.

I moved to the desk where Tommy had set up his navigation systems. The chart plotter was connected to a laptop computer. You could access sonar, radar, and GPS on either of the screens. I assumed that the system was also tied into the autopilot. I wanted to verify that, so I booted up the laptop. There was a blinking icon on the home screen. Out of curiosity, I clicked on it. A message came up.

If you can find it, give it to my mother. It's in the secret place. Not wet but wet. Not dry but dry.

"What the heck is that supposed to mean?" Bobby asked.

"I'm pretty sure I know what it means," I told him. "He showed me a little trick when I was last on this boat."

In the forward half of the boat, separate from the engine room, was another below-deck compartment. I lifted the hatch. It was full of water. I felt around underwater along the edge of the hatch opening. I found it. I flipped the switch and heard a pump come on. Tommy had rigged a small twelve-volt pump to evacuate the bilge space. There was a simple shutoff valve to refill it as necessary. The water was there to hide the waterproof container epoxied to the bilge floor. He told me it was something he had read about in a Travis McGee novel. I had a similar setup on *Leap of Faith*. I'd read the same book. My hatch was hidden under one of the V-berth bunks. I kept the space over it well crammed with assorted junk in order to discourage anyone for looking any further.

Bobby and I watched as the water drained out. The box had a key lock on it. I went to the helm and pulled the key out of the ignition. There were several more keys on the chain. Sure enough, one of them fit the box. Inside was a large stack of cash, wrapped in cellophane and sealed with wax.

"That's a lot of dough," said Bobby. "How does he know we won't keep it?"

"I think he assumed I'd be the one to find it," I said. "He trusts me. He showed me his hiding place, didn't he?"

"How could he know?"

"I told you he's a very smart guy," I said. "He's been in touch with Holly all this time. He knew I'd find her eventually."

"Why wouldn't he just give it to his mother himself?" he asked. "Before he ran."

"There was probably a lot of heat on her after he left," I suggested. "The Feds would have questioned her. Probably searched this boat as well."

"They would have turned on the laptop for sure," he said.

"Couldn't figure out the clue," I said. "Or the hiding spot."

"So we just take it back to her house?" he asked.

"In the dinghy," I said. "Won't take long."

The front of her house faced the street. The back faced the dock. I knocked on the back door. The old woman opened it a crack.

"I'm Tommy's friend," I said.

"I seen you here before," she said. "I ain't seen him before."

"He's with me," I said. "Tommy had us bring you something. You're going to want it."

I showed her the money. I hadn't counted it, but it looked to be at least ten grand.

"Tommy sent that for me?" she asked. "Where is he?"

"I can't tell you where he is," I said. "I'll be seeing him soon if you want me to get a message to him."

"You can tell that simple son of a bitch I could have used this money sooner," she said. "Damn near about to lose the house. I can catch up now. Tell him thanks for that I guess."

"Yes ma'am," I said.

"Tommy has always been a strange boy," she said. "But if you're his friend you probably know that. Smarter than a whip some ways, but dumber than a chunk in others. Off chasing treasure while his mother wastes away alone in this house. God damn G-men always sniffing around. Metal detectors in the yard and such. You know I didn't hear from him for ten years?"

"He was in jail for a part of that time," I said. "Hiding from the law the rest of it."

"I figured he was done with that life when he came here," she said. "Then that rust bucket boat shows up out back. I begged him to give up treasure hunting. He couldn't do it. Not even for his mom."

"Sorry ma'am," I said. "But we really should be going."

"You're taking that boat to Tommy ain't you?" she asked. "He's sniffing for gold someplace."

"I've already said too much," I said. "Take that money. Forget we were here."

"They're going to know the boat's missing," she said. "I'm old, not foolish. They'll be back around here."

"You don't know what happened to it," I said. "You woke up one day and it was gone."

"Good riddance," she said. "It was not only an eyesore, it was a constant reminder of where my Tommy went wrong."

"Come on, Breeze," said Bobby. "We've got to go. Nice meeting you ma'am."

"He's right," I said. "Sorry to bother you."

She closed the door. I could hear assorted chains and deadbolts going back into place. I felt sorry for her. Tommy had made and squandered millions, but his mother still owed money on her house. Maybe he was afraid that if he paid off her mortgage, the Feds would take it from her. I should have advised her not to plunk down the whole ten grand all at once, lest the bank wonder where it came from.

As we approached the old shrimper, I noticed that the rust had managed to conceal the name on either side of the bow. There never was a name on the transom. For the life of me, I couldn't recall the name of Tommy's boat. I really was slipping. It was such a simple thing. Age was catching up to me, no matter how hard I tried to deny it. I instructed Bobby to find a wire brush or other means of cleaning up the name plates. I didn't want the

Coast Guard to stop us for something so minor. I checked the running lights and anchor light while he worked. The name became visible. Tommy's boat was called *Coming Home*. That was the name it carried when Tommy bought it. The rust told me he hadn't bothered to change it.

I was satisfied that the old shrimper was ready for duty. We pulled up anchor and headed south for Marathon. We took on fuel and water at Pancho's. We anchored and got some groceries. We didn't need much. It would just be me onboard for three or four days. I didn't buy any beer or rum for the trip. I'd stay sharp and sober until we made it to safe harbor. I'd make Tommy buy me drinks after we arrived.

We left the next morning for Stock Island. I was happy with the boat's performance. The engine purred and all systems worked within their normal ranges. Everything felt right at a speed of nine knots. I calculated that the trip would be seven hundred miles to the mouth of the river. At nine knots, it would take seventy-eight hours to reach the shores of Guatemala. If the winds were favorable, Holly's boat could achieve the same nine knots. I knew she'd have to tack along the way, increasing the mileage she'd have to cover. We'd most likely get separated at some point. I couldn't waste the fuel following a crooked sailboat course across an open ocean.

Another Adventure was at anchor when we arrived. I was glad to see it. I didn't want to sit around for days waiting for Holly to finish diving with the tourists. *Coming Home* was an oddity in this anchorage. It really didn't belong. It would raise suspicion eventually. I'd been so occupied with logistics and familiarizing myself with Tommy's boat, I hadn't worried about how Holly would react to my arrival. We had a habit of leaving things unsaid whenever we departed. Our relationship was always about seeing what happens next. This trip promised to be one great big *we'll see what happens*.

Bobby and I boarded Holly's boat for a planning session. I introduced the two of them. Holly accepted Bobby without reservation. She was too trusting that way, but I'd brought him along. She had to assume that I approved of him. He hadn't been tested so far. He'd proven a quick learner, though. There was no way to judge how he'd react under pressure. I was really hoping for smooth seas. If things got hairy, I couldn't guarantee that he'd be capable crew for Holly. We sat down in front of Holly's GPS.

"I don't care what today's political situation is, or where the wind blows you, but stay well outside the twenty-mile line going around Cuba," I told Holly. "No shortcuts."

"Got it," she replied. "We go out and around Cuba. Where do I point towards after that?"

I scrolled the map down to Central America. At the southern tip of Belize, there was a spot called Punta Gorda, ironically enough. Punta Gorda, Florida had been home base for me when I first bought my boat. I pointed it out to Holly and Bobby.

"Aim for this point," I said. "This is Amatique Bay. It looks like it will provide some shelter if we need it before entering the river. The river mouth is here, at Livingston."

"How far upriver are the marinas?" Holly asked.

"It's about eighteen miles," I said. "We go through this lake called El Golfete first."

"Where do we anchor?" she asked.

"It looks like there's a choice of spots," I said. "We need land access to get to Tommy. I'd guess outside of one of the marinas would work. Can you Google it?"

She worked her phone for a solid twenty minutes. There were plenty of options, but we had special needs. We didn't want to draw too much attention. We needed enough water for Holly's six-foot draft. We needed access to goods and services as necessary. Finally, she made a decision.

"Here, in Texan Bay," she said. It's in Cayo Quemodo, at the entrance to El Golfete. It's an anchorage and a marina, run by Americans. It's out of the way somewhat, but they say it has a launch that will take you to Livingston or Rio Dulce for supplies."

"Americans?" I asked.

"Here, read this," she said. "Mike and Sherri Payne are from Texas. Hence, Texan Bay."

"It looks perfect," I said. "Good job."

"All you need is a phone," she said. "Anyone can do it. Modern technology and whatnot."

"I'll admit that a phone is very useful," I said. "Doesn't mean I'm getting one."

My two friends looked at me like I'd just stepped out of the eighteenth century. No one could understand how I could go through life without a phone. Apparently, I was the last person on the planet that didn't own one. Holly and I had been through this conversation more than once. It would be so simple for me to just call her up, if and when I wanted to find her. I understood that, but there was more to it. I'd been hunted more than once. A phone was the easiest way to be found. I didn't have an ATM card either. Most of the time, I didn't want to be found. There was a great big crazy world out there that I knew little about. I didn't care to know. I didn't know the ballplayer's names. I didn't know who the top singers or actors were. Occasionally, I'd catch a whiff of politics in some bar. It seemed to invade everything. Donald Trump was the president, I knew that much. Half the people loved him and half the people hated him. A few years back, while investigating some Russian mobsters, I came across his name in connection with one of his resorts. The locals called it Little Moscow. A bunch of Russian bad guys had bought property from the Trump organization, after the fall of the Soviet Union.

I'd also had some dealings with Florida's Attorney General, Pam Bondi. My ex-lawyer and ex-lover was able to pay her a bribe to squash an investigation. Later I learned that Bondi had been accused of accepting campaign donations from Trump, in exchange for dropping an investigation into his university. Nothing came out of it. It was all politics as usual. I had no need for it in my life. All the players seemed like crooks to me, regardless of political affiliation. What I couldn't figure out, was how two seemingly rational thinking people could see things so differently. When political talk broke out in bars, it was always the same thing. One guy saw black and the other guy saw white. Normal people would go mad trying to explain why each other was wrong. It was my understanding that the internet was full of hatred coming from all directions. I sure as hell didn't need that in my life. I could survive without a phone, thank you very much.

"Don't let him rub off on you, Bobby," Holly said. "He still chases dinosaurs with a club."

"He's got some pretty nice electronics on his boat," Bobby said. "He uses that newfangled GPS with satellites and everything."

"You should probably be navigating by the stars, Breeze," she said. "The Feds might track you by your chart plotter."

"As far as I know, they'd have to physically place a device on my boat to track me," I said. "For that, they'd have to find me first."

"I'd advise staying off their radar in the first place," she said.

"Shit happens," I said. "The last time they were after me, was because I was covering for you. Remember?"

"You're right," she said. "I was just teasing you. Let's move this conversation to a different topic."

"Seventy-eight hours at nine knots," I said. "That's to the mouth of the river."

"Should we rendezvous outside in that bay?" she asked.

"Depends on the weather," I said. "Which is your department. What do you have?"

"Almost smooth sailing," she said. "Perfect for me."

"Almost smooth?" asked Bobby. "What's that mean exactly?"

"*Another Adventure* needs some wind to make her fly," she explained. "It won't be flat out there, but we can keep up with Breeze in a good wind. Maybe beat him if it holds up the whole way."

"Sounds sporty," he said. "What will I have to do?"

"Take watch so I can sleep," she said. "Wake me if something goes wonky."

"That's it?"

"I'll teach you the rest," she said. "It's three days and a little bit at sea. It'll be fun."

"Holly's idea of fun might not be the same as your idea of fun," I said to Bobby. "We need to know that you're committed to this. It's not a pleasure cruise."

"I'd be better off behind the wheel of Tommy's boat," he said.

"Tommy expects Breeze to run his boat," Holly said. "Breeze is good with power boats, real good. Tommy trusts him. It was his hope all along that it would be Breeze making the delivery."

"I guess I better learn to sail real quick," Bobby said.

"Holly is a good teacher," I told him. "If she can teach me, she can teach you."

"Bobby the sailor man," said Holly. "I'll have you flying from a spinnaker before I'm done with you."

We punched coordinates into Holly's GPS. She said she was fueled and provisioned. The weather forecast was good. The trip was a go. There was no point in delaying it. I left Bobby with Holly and went back to *Coming Home* alone. I needed a good night's sleep. I wouldn't get a decent amount of rest until we were safely in Texan Harbor. I lay down on Tommy's pathetic cot and tried to decipher Holly's attitude towards me. There was no relationship talk. She was focused on the mission. Bobby was there. She'd been friendly to us both, but nothing more. I'd just have to wait and see what would happen. In the meantime, I had a boat to drive a very long way.

I went over the course from Key West to Guatemala in my head before falling asleep.

Nine

In the morning, I hailed Holly on the radio. I tried her preferred channel first. She liked to use seventy-two for idle chatter. Sure enough, she was monitoring it.

"Another Adventure, Another Adventure. This is Coming Home."

"Go ahead *Coming Home*", she replied.

"Is the weather still good?" I asked.

"Damn near perfect," she said. "Unless something drastic happens, we've got a good four-day window. Should be just like this all the way."

"Is our crew member ready to roll?" I asked.

"We're both ready," she said. "Waiting on you, old man."

"I was watching Lawrence Welk from my wheelchair," I said. "Lost track of time."

"Hobble on over to the helm," she said. "Let's blow this popcorn stand."

"Last one there is a rotten egg," I said.

"You're on."

I fired up the big diesel and raised anchor as quickly as I could. I made a fast pass by Holly's boat, throwing a big wake. Bobby was on his way forward when the wake caught him off guard. He fell but managed not to go overboard. I laughed as loudly as I could in his direction. Holly shrugged. She followed me as we motored out through the Boca Chica Channel. Once in open water, Holly's sails went up. We cut across the Key West Ship Channel, over Eastern Dry Rocks, and south of Sand Key. We turned into the Southwest Channel and pointed our bows towards big water.

The wind was out of the east at close to fifteen knots. Seas ranged from three to five feet. The heavy steel hull under my feet was unperturbed by the waves. *Another Adventure* sliced along like a playful dolphin. That old familiar feeling came over me. There was simply nothing like taking a boat out on the ocean. I knew Holly was feeling it too. Bobby was probably scared shitless. I hoped that he'd grow some real sea legs in a hurry. If not, he'd be a hindrance to Holly instead of a helping hand.

Three days and a little bit, I told myself. Guatemala, here we come. I stayed at the helm for twenty straight hours. I maintained the targeted nine knots all day. The gauges remained in their normal range. I learned the boat's sounds. I felt her rhythm. Holly was off to my west a few miles. We wanted to stay in visual contact if possible, but we didn't want to stay so close that we'd get in each other's way. She might tack while I was taking a nap. I radioed to her before going to sleep. Bobby answered. He was on his first solo watch. Holly and I would be asleep at the same time, leaving our fate in Bobby's hands. I was too tired to worry about it.

"Just stay awake, Bobby," I said. "Wake us up if something even looks funny."

"I'm good," he said. "I learned a lot today. I had a good nap. Go ahead and rest."

I was awakened by the crackle of the radio. I didn't know how long I'd been asleep.

"*Leap of Faith, Leap...*shit...*Coming Home, Coming Home.* Wake up Breeze."

It was Holly. I asked her what was going on.

"We've been watching a blip on the radar," she said. "Looks like we'll pass on either side of it."

"Is it moving?" I asked.

"Maybe," she said. "Hard to tell. We think it's drifting west slightly."

"See any lights yet?"

"No, but we should be able to make them out by now," she said. "One mile in front of us."

"I advise caution," I said. "Do we even need to approach it?"

"What if it's Cubans or something?" she asked.

"I doubt a Cuban raft would show up on radar," I said. "It's something bigger. Maybe a shipping container."

"I want to move in closer," she said. "Let's get a look at it anyway. If it's junk we'll just keep on sailing."

I wiped the sleep from my eyes and adjusted course slightly. I stared ahead into the darkness. I saw nothing. When we were on top of the radar blip, Holly shone a spotlight on the object. It was a sailboat. There didn't appear to be anyone on board. The sails had been left up, but only tatters remained. The vessel must have been abandoned unless the captain was still on board but dead. Pulling alongside and attempting to board would be extremely dangerous. I could think of nothing that could be done.

"It's *Hooten Holler*," said Holly over the radio. "It was all the talk in Key West and Marathon about a month ago."

"What happened to it?" I asked.

"The husband got hit in the head and went overboard," she said. "He was tethered but the wife was unable to get him back on deck."

"That's awful," I said. "What happened to her?"

"Coast Guard picked them both up," she said. "But it was too rough to take the boat in tow. They left it floating about seventy-five miles south of the Dry Tortugas."

"What were they doing out there?"

"Heading to Mexico," she said. "Damn shame."

"A sober reminder not to take the sea for granted," I told her. "Nothing we can do here."

"Didn't hurt to check," she said.

"You going back to sleep?" I asked.

"It will be daylight soon," she said. "I'm good. I'll send Bobby down to rest. You okay?"

"I got about three hours," I said. "It will have to do for now."

We left the abandoned sailboat behind us and continued south. It made me sad to think about it. That poor woman lost her husband, her boat, and her dreams. I sent up a silent prayer, asking for the safety of my vessel and Holly's.

"For life and death are one, even as the river and the sea are one."

Khalil Gibran

Holly drifted off to the west to regain our separation. I chugged along at nine knots all that day, taking catnaps from time to time. Over the radio, we decided to time our rest periods so that either Holly or I would be awake. Bobby had done nothing wrong on his solo watch, but there was no point in giving too much responsibility to a novice. Finding that boat adrift was an eerie feeling. I could sense the tension over on *Another Adventure*. I felt it too. The last time I'd made a similar crossing, I had two crew members to take shifts. We'd run to Columbia and returned with a hold full of pure cocaine. I was still living off that money, and probably would for the rest of my life. I wasn't proud of it, but the money gave me the freedom I so desperately desired.

We stayed on our toes throughout the next night and all of the next day. Then the wind died. Holly fell back. I continued on. We had a contingency plan for just this situation. If it remained calm, I'd wait offshore of Punta Gorda. If it was rough, I'd go into El Golfete and wait there. On the third night, there was no wind whatsoever. I was far out in front of Holly, though we still had radio contact. We debated whether or not she should fire up her engine. In the end, she decided to run it for a few hours, and hope the wind picked up again.

It did. Just after sunrise on our last day, the wind roared out of the east. The seas built rapidly. The waves helped drop my speed to eight knots. Holly would be flying, but it would be a wild ride. I pictured Bobby wearing a life jacket, huddled up and hanging on for dear life. The radio crackled to life.

"Woohoo!" yelled Holly. "We're coming for you, Breeze. Fourteen knots and ripping."

"I'm going to angle in close to the coast," I said. "I want to get out of this wind."

"Sissy stink potter," she said. "If you go too far out of your way, I'll pass you."

"Go ahead, girl," I said. "I'm tired. Let's anchor somewhere south of Punta Gorda. We'll be in the lee and we can all get some sleep."

I turned the rusty old shrimper towards Belize. I steered the boat to hit the waves at a forty-five-degree angle. Her sharp prow sliced into the sea. I kept angling inshore until the ride smoothed out. I paralleled the coast, working my way south again. Holly's sails came into view off to my east. She'd caught up and then some. The only way I could win this race was to hurry up and find a spot to drop anchor. Originally, I wanted to get close to Livingston before stopping. I was only halfway down the coast of Guatemala when I pulled up. I turned inshore and crept along until the bottom came up. Once I had a reasonable depth to drop anchor in, I let it go.

"What are you doing?" said Holly over the radio. "I thought we were going further south."

"I'm beat," I said. "My anchor's down. I win."

"You cheated," she said. "I demand an official inquiry."

"Come on in here," I said. "It's pretty calm. You can file your complaint with the race official later. His name is Breeze."

"It's a conspiracy I tell you," she said, laughing.

It was good to hear her laugh. We'd shaken the funk that the lost sailboat had brought upon us. We'd made it, almost, to our destination. The hard part was over. I watched *Another Adventure* fall off the wind as it turned towards me. The sails came down. Holly brought her vessel within a hundred yards and dropped her anchor.

"Nighty night," she said. "We're beat too, but we made it."

"We'll regroup after the last one of us wakes up," I said. "Sweet dreams."

I did not have sweet dreams. The doors tried to come back. I just caught a glimpse of them. My subconscious mind worked to make them disappear. I wanted no part of those doors. I woke up with a foreboding feeling. Was something bad waiting for us up that river? I wanted a beer but I remembered that I hadn't brought any. Tommy was going to have a big bar tab when I caught up with him. There was no sign of life on *Another Adventure* yet. I made myself something to eat and looked over the chart plotter. We had another hour to get to the mouth of the river, then maybe one more hour to Texan Bay. It would be a relief to finish off this final leg.

When I saw Holly and Bobby moving about, I took the dinghy over to them. Holly's deck and rigging were covered in salt. So were Holly and Bobby. They were in good spirits, though.

"Those last few hours were awesome," Holly said. "My old boat was a rocket. So much fun."

"What about you, Bobby?" I asked. "Was it fun for you too?"

"At first I was terrified," he said. "But watching Holly emboldened me. She was so excited. I just went with it. Not sure I'd call it fun, but I overcame."

"Her and this boat are really something when the wind is up," I said. "Sailing is in her blood."

"I'm not ready to trade my tug in just yet," he said.

"Stink potters," said Holly.

We sat and talked until sunset. Holly and Bobby were comfortable together. I was comfortable too, but wished Bobby wasn't there at that moment. I wondered if I'd ever get to have a heart to heart with Holly. Soon we'd add a fourth person to our merry band of pirates. I didn't want to go treasure hunting. Bobby would want to return to his boat. I might be only a few days away from a plane ride back to Florida.

I left them as darkness set in. There were no lights from shore. We were far enough out that the bugs didn't bother us. I got a good night's sleep. I just turned off all the worries and shut my brain down. I needed it.

We were all itching to move at first light. Everyone was rested and eager. We eased our way into the river. High bluffs rose on either side. The gorge rose up almost three hundred feet above us on both sides. Mahogany and palms lined the banks. Howler monkeys swung amongst the wildflowers. It was beautiful and primitive. We came out into the lake and looked for the marina known as Texan Bay. I hovered around outside the docks, trying to get a look at things, before anchoring out in the center of the basin. The rusty old shrimp boat now dominated the local landscape. Holly anchored nearby.

We barely had time to shut down our engines when a skiff came out to greet us. A big gruff looking fellow introduced himself as Mike Payne. He was the owner of the marina, along with his wife Sherri. He was mostly bald, with a white mustache and plenty of white stubble on his face. He was large and still in decent shape for his age. My first impression was that he was a menacing figure, but when he spoke he came across as kind. His Texas drawl was thick and most likely a bit exaggerated.

"My name's Breeze," I said. "That's Holly and Bobby over there."

"Welcome to Texan Bay," he said. "This old rust bucket is a bit large for these parts."

"I thought it would be less crowded and I'd be less of a hazard here," I said. "But I'll gladly accept other suggestions."

"You'll be okay here," he said. "Come on in and meet the missus once you get settled in. We'll fix you up some barbecue."

"That sound great," I said. "We've been eating sandwiches for three days."

"Where'd you come in from?"

"Stock Island," I said. "I'm delivering this boat. The girl on that sailboat plans to stay awhile."

"Whose boat is it?" he asked.

"I'm not sure I'm supposed to say," I told him. "He'll have to come claim it soon enough."

"If he decides to keep it here, I'll be needing to know who he is," he said. "We try to keep the shady business to a minimum."

"I understand," I said. "As soon as we get in touch with him, I'll let him know."

"Sherri can get you into town if you need to get a phone or a SIM card," he said.

"You've been very helpful," I said.

He went off to introduce himself to Holly and Bobby. His kindness seemed genuine, but I wouldn't want to have to tangle with him. I figured that he didn't become king of his little kingdom without being tough. I vowed to do my best to stay on his good side.

It felt good to have reached our destination in one piece. The trip had gone as good as could be expected. I didn't know how Holly planned to get in touch with Tommy. I didn't know where he was holed up. I did know that he was pretty good at not being found. After swindling his investors out of millions, he'd stayed underground for years. It was only by a freak accident that the Feds got a lead on his whereabouts. If he would have revealed the location of his gold, he could have avoided jail. He chose to do the time. Now he was on the run again. Guatemala was a long way from the Florida Keys. It seemed like as good a place to hide as any, but Tommy didn't choose it for that. He chose it as a base to hunt for treasure. It was always about the treasure for Tommy. I'd had enough of treasure hunting.

I watched Big Mike leave Holly and Bobby and head back into the marina. I put the dinghy in the water and went over to them. Holly was doing a little dance on deck.

"We made it, Breeze," she said. "We're here."

"Good trip," I said. "You good, Bobby?"

"I'm great," he said. "This place looks awesome."

"And the owner seemed real nice," said Holly. "Let's go in and get something to eat."

"And a cold beer," said Bobby.

"I'll drink to that," I said. "How do we get in touch with Tommy?"

"I've got to call him," she said. "He gave me a Guatemalan number, but I'll need to borrow a local phone or get a SIM card for mine."

"Big Mike said his wife could help with that," I said. "He also wants to know who owns the shrimper. I'm guessing he keeps close tabs on things here."

"Let's talk to Tommy before we say anything," she said. "His call."

We all loaded into my dinghy and made our way to the docks. A slim, curly-haired woman came trotting down the pier. She wore a loose-fitting sundress that flapped with the motion of her arms. I thought she was in an unnecessary hurry, but I soon learned that she galloped about wherever she went. Sherri greeted us. Her little dog greeted us too. His name was Ima, as in Ima Payne.

"You're too soon for barbecue," she said. "But we can throw some burgers on the grill."

"Cold beer?" I asked. "I'd kiss you and the dog for some cold beer."

"Aren't you the charmer?" she said. "And I'll take that kiss right now before you back out of the deal."

She planted a big wet one right on my lips.

"Welcome to Texan Bay, honey," she said, smiling from ear to ear. "Mike's got plenty of beer in the cooler up there. Have a seat in the shade, all of you."

We sat at long wooden tables on the porch. The area was adorned with an assortment of flags and nautical items. Mike brought three ice cold beers to the table. I drank half of mine in one slug. It was the coldest, best-tasting beer I'd ever had.

"Nectar of the Gods," I said. "Thanks so much."

I knew that Holly rarely drank anymore, but I watched her chug half her beer.

"Yup," she said. "Nectar of the Gods."

We waited for Bobby to take a long drink of his beer, then we all clinked our bottles together in celebration.

"To the Gods," we said.

Mike kept bringing the beers and we kept drinking them. The conversation flowed. We ate burgers that must have weighed a pound each. Mike and Sherri treated us like old friends. Holly used Sherri's phone to call Tommy. She walked down to the docks to get some privacy. When she came back I asked about the call.

"He's in the village at Rio Dulce," she said. "He's looking for a ride here. Should be able to make it tomorrow."

"There's been some trouble up there," said Mike. "Makes us glad to be down here."

"What kind of trouble?" I asked.

"It started out as petty theft," he said. "Then outboards and dinghies started to disappear. The thieves have basically become a gang now. The locals are pretty tense."

"Any law enforcement?" I asked.

"They patrol the harbor at night," he said. "They keep the cruisers safe, but leave the village to its own means."

"Sounds like it might cause some resentment," I said.

"The locals depend on the cruisers," he said. "They understand where their bread is buttered."

"Why the thefts then?"

"The gang is made up of young men from the hills," he said. "The poverty level here is absolutely crushing. The country was in a civil war for their entire lives until recently. They used to have the Resistance to sustain them. Now they have nothing."

"The Resistance?"

"The government was beyond corrupt and controlled by the military," he explained. "The working people, farmers, and tradesmen, rose up in rebellion. Every leader that was overthrown was replaced by one even more corrupt."

"What happened to the rebellion?" I asked.

"It was put down," he said. "Thousands died. Things have stabilized now. Many of the corrupt leaders have been jailed or are in exile. There is no cause to fight anymore. The young ones get restless."

"Third World politics," I said.

"You can't escape politics," he said. "Not even in Paradise."

"I'm learning that more and more," I said.

As I talked with Mike, Holly and Bobby talked with Sherri. They were discussing the trip down and their plans now that they'd arrived. I heard Bobby say he might want to stick around for a while. Holly sounded excited about her adventures to come. I was not part of their discussion. Why would I be? I was supposed to fly back to Florida soon. I'd meet with Tommy and turn over possession of his boat first. He was supposed to pay me for my efforts and buy me a ticket home.

I rounded up my crew and made the call to return to our boats. I didn't want to wear out the Texan's hospitality on our first night. I paid cash for the burgers and beers, patted Ima Payne on the head, and said good night. I dropped Holly and Bobby at *Another Adventure* and went to the shrimper alone. Being alone was one thing. Knowing that Bobby was over there with Holly was another. I was starting to think that bringing him along was a mistake.

With my belly full of burger and beer, sleep came easily. The floating doors did not torment me. No little angels lectured me on my behavior. The harbor was silent. I slept like the dead.

The next day we met some of the other cruisers at the marina. Everyone wanted to talk to Holly. She instantly became the queen of the marina. I sat in the shade sipping water, waiting for Tommy to arrive. He showed up late in the afternoon.

"I knew you'd come through for me, Breeze," he said.

"How'd you know it would be me to bring the boat down here?" I asked.

"I've been talking with Holly all along," he said. "If you hadn't shown up, she'd have tracked you down sooner or later."

"You think you've got a shot at some more treasure down here?" I asked.

"I've got wrecks…lots of them" he said. "I've been doing some research, going through old archives and such. I'm trying to narrow the field. Some of them are too deep. Some of them were carrying grain. It's a big puzzle I'm trying to sort out."

"Where do you start?" I asked.

"I'm going to do a survey," he said. "Run out there and make some waypoints. Get a feel for what we've got. You should come along."

"How long?"

"A week or so," he said. "Bunch of potential sites to catalog."

"All of us on your boat for a week?"

"We'll have to improve the accommodations, of course," he said.

"Mike here can probably get us some hammocks or mattresses," I suggested.

"Can you take care of that for me?" he asked, handing me a wad of bills.

"Sure," I said. "I guess so. You'll need to meet him. He has to know who owns the boat."

"Is he a straight shooter?"

"I just met him yesterday," I said. "But he seems like a good guy."

"I can't have everyone knowing what I'm up to," he said. "Those punks in Rio Dulce will be all over me."

"What's going on up there?" I asked.

"Criminals I tell you," he said. "They're getting too bold. Everything has to stay locked up, and sometimes that's not enough. Nobody will come out after dark. Purse snatching, shoplifting, bullying. They are ruining life in Rio Dulce."

"Where's your money?"

"I pulled up some floorboards and buried it in the dirt," he said. "No one knows I've got diddly."

"We'll need to transfer it to the boat," I said.

"I'm going to need your help with that," he said. "And any other help I can get."

"I've got Bobby," I said. "Big Mike would be a huge help if he'd agree to it."

"That's four of us," he said.

"How many of these punks are roaming the streets?"

"Usually three or four at a time," he said. "But they could muster a dozen if they knew something was up."

"Guns?" I asked.

"Haven't seen any," he said. "Guns would bring the law down on them. So far, no one seems to care."

"We can deal with three or four unarmed punks," I said. "Let's hope the odds don't get any worse than that. Keep a low profile. Don't act like anything is out of the ordinary."

"I've been doing that since I got here," he said.

I went off to tell Bobby and try to recruit Big Mike. Bobby didn't flinch. The trip down from Florida had given him some confidence. I could see the change in him. The old Bobby would have been a puppy dog at Holly's side every minute, pining for affection, like he'd done with Jennifer. Now he was ready to stand up to gangsters and go off searching for treasure.

Mike was a different story. He had legitimate reasons to not want to get involved.

"I've got to consider the safety of this place," he explained. "If we bust up some punks in Rio Dulce, the next thing you know they'll be down here stealing shit and harassing my customers."

"With you along, they might decide not to cause any trouble for us," I suggested. "Strength is deterrence."

"If that's the case, then just walk down the street waving shotguns," he said. "They'd scatter like the rats they are."

"Attention we don't need," I said.

"Look, I've busted some heads in my day," he said. "I'm not afraid to mix it up with some kids that are stealing purses, but unless you want to take care of the problem once and for all, I'm out."

"What do you mean, once and for all?"

"Run them out of town," he said. "Teach them all a lesson. Bring stability back to the town."

"That's a lot more than I bargained for," I said.

"Me too," he said. "But it's going to come to that sooner or later."

"I should be sitting on a beach in Florida by then," I said.

"I'll get you a fast boat to run up there in," he said. "Anything else you need, but I'm staying put. Sorry."

"I understand," I said. "And thanks."

Ten

Mike hooked us up with a sporty looking Panga, a modest-sized, open boat popular throughout Central America. It was powered by a big Mercury outboard.

"She'll run in the mid-forties comfortably," he said. "Gas tank is full. You can top if off when you get back."

"It's great," I said. "Really more than necessary. Thanks."

Tommy and Bobby met me at the dock. It was a nice day for a boat ride. Tommy carried an empty duffel bag so that he could pack some clothes. He said that the money was already in another duffel. We just had to brush the dirt off. He had a history of storing cash underground. He paid rent on a fancy rental property in the Keys with mildewed bills while hiding from the Feds. We all boarded the Panga. I drove. We ran up the river to Rio Dulce.

"Tommy packs his clothes," I said to Bobby. "You and I pull up the floorboards and get the other duffel. Clean it up real good. A dirt covered bag will draw attention."

"Tie up at Mar Marine," said Tommy. "My shack is next to Ranchon Mary."

"I don't know the area," I said. "You'll have to guide us."

"We'll come to a big point before the bridge," he said. "Mar Marine is on the east edge of the point. Ranchon Mary is a restaurant on the water's edge up in the cove."

"Can't we tie up there?" I asked.

"The boat will be safe at Mar," he said. "It's a so-called yacht club. No one will bother it there."

"How far is the walk?"

"Quarter mile or so," he said. "Not far, but right through town."

"It's broad daylight," said Bobby. "Maybe we'll waltz right through."

"Stay alert," I told him. "Remember what I told you."

"Got it," he said. "Head on a swivel."

Tommy pointed to a row of docks just beyond the point. We tied up in an open slip. Tommy handed what passes for a dock attendant a twenty, telling him we wouldn't be long. All three of us walked up to the street and headed towards Tommy's shack. Ranchon Mary was a sprawling complex of high thatched roofs along a makeshift seawall. There was a marina just across the waterway. The restaurant wasn't open yet. If it was, Tommy said, we could have probably tied up there as customers. I didn't want to hang around long enough to eat lunch. He opened the heavy padlock on the only entrance to his humble abode. He'd be living large on his boat, compared to this hovel. We closed it behind us and got straight to work.

Bobby and I recovered the money bearing duffel. It was moist and smelled strongly of earth and mildew. We tried to towel if off with little success. It had a light green fuzz that was firmly adhered to the fabric. Tommy finished packing. Bobby snuck a look out the door. The street was clear. The money duffel stuck out. It couldn't have been worse unless it had a sign on it saying "Money Inside."

"It's only seven or eight blocks," Bobby said. "We didn't see any signs of trouble on the way here."

"They may have seen us," I said. "They could be watching to see what we'll do. Three gringos carrying bags."

"Breeze is right," said Tommy. "We came in with one empty bag. We're leaving with two full ones. We'll be a curiosity at least."

"Let's do what we came to do," I said. "Walk normally, but don't waste any time."

We went out the door and started making our way back to the boat. We managed to travel three blocks before being confronted. Three dark-skinned young men, maybe twenty years old, stood in our path. They spoke in a language I didn't understand.

"Is that Spanish?" I asked Tommy.

"It's sort of a mix of Spanish and some kind of Mayan dialect," he said. "They understand Spanish though I reckon."

"Do you?"

He spoke to them in Spanish. The tallest of the three responded.

"They want to know what's in the bags," he said.

"Clothes and personal stuff," I said. "Ask them to step aside."

They exchanged a few more sentences. I understood almost none of it. I did understand body language. These three were going to look in our bags, whether we allowed it or not. I sized them up. They looked malnourished, which could lead to desperation. They were all wiry, but didn't look particularly athletic. They were slow and unaware. I couldn't tell due to the language barrier, but I guessed they weren't too smart. Tommy and Bobby looked to me for a clue as to what to do.

The tall one reached for the money bag. I snatched him by the arm, spun him around and kicked him in the ass.

"No," I said.

That was his last warning. He took one step towards me and I dropped him with a hard right.

"Tommy, go to the boat now," I yelled. "Bobby stay here."

I kicked my victim while he was down. He curled up in a ball. The other two went after Bobby. He blocked a few weak punches before gut-punching the smaller one. We both confronted the last thug. He backed away with his hands out in front of him. He'd seen enough. All it took was a little resistance and the punks folded. We continued on our way without further disturbance. A little black girl pulled back a curtain and smiled at me through the window. I waved.

Tommy was waiting anxiously. He had the motor running. Bobby and I hopped aboard and untied the lines. I kept it at a slow idle until we cleared the docks. As soon as it was prudent, I jammed the throttle forward and we sped away from the village. As we approached the docks of Texan Bay, Tommy and Bobby lifted the duffels up above their heads for all to see. Scattered applause and cheers came from the onlookers. Our mission was a success. I topped off the fuel tank and thanked Mike again. I brought Tommy over for a little sit-down. I sought out a beer while they talked. If Tommy wanted to use Texan Bay as a home base for his operation, he'd have to come to some sort of mutual agreement with the proprietor.

Bobby ran the duffel bags out to the old shrimper. He picked up Holly on the way back. We all sat in the shade, enjoying the afternoon. Tommy paid for our drinks. Eventually, the conversation turned to his upcoming enterprise. The big question was how many of us would participate. Bobby and I had boats to return to. I was considering going on the cataloging tour of the wrecks Tommy had identified. I was not interested in partnering with him to actually dive for gold. Holly was dead-set on helping him. She had her boat. She had no obligations elsewhere. It was why she was in Guatemala. Holly grilled Bobby on his diving experience, which turned out to be minimal. He didn't have much mechanical experience on his resume either. He'd be a badly needed third set of hands, but he'd need to be quick on the learning curve. I was surprised that he was entertaining the idea of staying.

"What about your boat?" I asked him.

"Maybe I could hire you to bring it down here," he said.

"Not interested," I said. "No way, no how."

"Why not?"

"Your boat is too small for starters," I said. "Plus every time you cross an ocean you're tempting fate. If I cross another one, it will be in my own boat."

"You thinking about bringing *Leap of Faith* down here?" asked Holly.

"I wasn't," I said. "Just keeping my options open."

"That's the great thing about living on a boat," she said. "Options are practically unlimited."

I kept waiting for some sign that Holly actually wanted me to stay in Guatemala. It never came. She wasn't pushing me away, but she wasn't begging me to stay either. She seemed more interested in the prospect of Bobby joining the crew. Tommy simply knew that they needed at least a third crew member. He didn't seem to care which person it was, as long as they could be trusted. I had airfare home whenever I decided to leave.

"So what's the deal with these wrecks?" I asked him. "Where are they?"

"Mostly outside the reef near Belize," he said. "That's where I want to start."

"Isn't that super deep water?" I asked.

"Yes and no," he said. "There's actually a second reef out beyond the one everyone knows about. It's the world's largest double barrier reef. Beyond that, there are scattered coral atolls. The depths around those are manageable for a diver."

"Don't the dive boats go out there with tourists?"

"It's pure open water out there," he said. "There is no protection outside that second reef. It takes a skilled and experienced diver to work around the atolls. Not something most tourists are capable of."

"Are you comfortable with that Holly?" I asked.

She shrugged.

"I've got a magnetometer and side scan sonar," Tommy said. "We study the sites from above the surface thoroughly before we ever send her down. Keep the hazards to a minimum."

"Tommy says there are literally hundreds of wrecks out there," said Holly.

"How do you decide where to start?"

"At first I discounted the English merchant ships," he said. "I was looking for Spanish galleons that might have been carrying gold. I learned that several English ships went down with a hold full of silver. The biggest was the HMS Triumvirate. It went down near St. Georges Caye in 1787. I've been sorting through a lot of lore and legend. The Spanish kept excellent records, but I don't have access to them."

"You got weather and depth to be concerned about," I said. "What else seems problematic?"

"The Mexican Navy," he said. "They tend to investigate boats like mine near their waters."

"Permits required?" I asked.

"Required but impossible to get," he said. "You'd have to bribe half the government of two countries."

"Illegal dive operation in rough, deep water," I said. "Not my idea of a good time."

"I ain't scared," Holly said. "I'm excited."

"More power to you," I said. "I think it's crazy."

"I've been called crazy for most of my life," Tommy said. "Until I found the SS Central American."

"And tons of gold," I said. "How much was really down there, Tommy?"

"Ship's manifest said thirty thousand pounds," he said. "We didn't get it all."

"But you still have the itch," I said. "And you've infected Holly."

"I think I'm catching the bug too," Bobby said. "All this talk of sunken treasure is getting to me."

"I guess I'm immune," I said. "I'll help you with the initial survey, but count me out after that."

"Good," said Holly. "You can help Bobby get acclimated if he decides to stay."

"It's just for a week, right Tommy?" I asked.

"Give or take a few days," he said. "We'll drag the magnetometer outside the reef and along the atolls. I'll record everything the sonar sees. We'll sort out the hits and match up anything interesting with the sonar record later."

"No diving?" I asked.

"Not unless something just jumps out at us," he said. "Not likely. If it was easy to find someone would have already found it."

"What makes you certain that you'll be the one to find something out there?" I asked.

"It's what I do, Breeze," he said. "It's what I do."

I knew just what he meant. I could find people and figure things out. It's what I did. Tommy could find gold.

We spent two days rigging up sleeping arrangements and provisioning. Tommy explained how his new equipment worked. Bobby and I would deploy what was basically a towable metal detector. Tommy would drive the boat and watch the sonar screens. Holly would be at the helm, ready to make a waypoint if we got a hit. She and Tommy would study the results which were constantly being transferred to a laptop.

We left at first light. We entered Amatique Bay at Livingston and turned north towards the coast of Belize. The Caribbean Sea was calm, but we didn't expect it to stay that way. Before reaching the reef line, we slowed and put out the magnetometer. We experimented with the amount of cable to play out. We tried several different depths until Tommy was happy with it. He'd entered his target sites into the GPS. Then we trolled over them hoping to hear the alarm that signified metal content. It was tedious and boring.

We slowly worked a grid pattern over the GPS marks for three days. Nothing got Tommy's heart racing. He spent endless hours at the wheel, with his eyes glued to the sonar screen. Occasionally, I'd spell him so he could get some sleep. When the rest of us had nothing to do, we napped in hammocks or on an old mattress thrown in a corner. There was nothing glamorous about that part of treasure hunting.

We had no showers. Holly had put a box of baby wipes in Tommy's miserable head so we could take a whore bath. When it rained, we all ran out on deck to get rinsed off. Holly still looked nice even with salt encrusted skin and wrinkly clothes. Bobby had a black beard growing. Mine was mostly gray.

I started to notice a few peculiar behaviors from Bobby. He never rested when I did. It was as if he was trying to make a point about having more stamina. He wore his ability to stay awake longer as a badge of honor. Of course, that meant he was spending more and more time with Holly. He took an interest in the sonar scans and asked Tommy a lot of questions. He was really getting into the finer aspects of hunting for gold. I was just along for the ride. The three of them were ever vigilant, while I spent more and more time out on deck by myself. I still hadn't gotten a chance to talk to Holly alone. I missed my boat. I missed Pelican Bay. I was bored and irritable.

On day four, we got a serious hit. A cheer went up from the helm. Holly marked the spot. Then a series of smaller chirps were heard. We had passed over something that was metallic and large. It was surrounded by smaller pieces of metal.

"I'm going to bring her around for another pass," said Tommy.

"Now we're talking," Holly said.

"What do you think it is?" Bobby asked.

"All we know is that it is metal," said Tommy. "Could be a cannon, with some scattered hardware. Could be an old cook stove for all we know. Burners and racks lying around it."

We made another, slower pass. Tommy watched the sonar. We got the hit again, a few small beeps and one long one. Holly studied the sonar too. Something was down there, in forty feet of water. It was covered in marine growth. It did not look like a cook stove. We circled the site, making waypoints as we went. We went over it from east to west and from north to south. All of the information we captured was sent to the laptop. Finally, we veered off. Tommy had me pull in the magnetometer. Once we got closer to shore, we dropped anchor. Holly and Tommy poured over the laptop images.

"It's worth a closer look," Tommy said. "This will be where we start."

"Are you good with diving to forty feet?" I asked Holly.

"It's a little deep, but I've been down further," she said.

"It's gold," Bobby said. "I can feel it."

"Keep your hopes in check," said Tommy. "That way you won't be disappointed when we pull up a washing machine."

"Just thinking positive," Bobby said.

"You wouldn't believe the stuff I've seen down there," Tommy said. "Cars, barges, shipping containers. Even found a sextant once."

"How many false alarms have you investigated?" asked Holly.

"Hundreds," said Tommy. "You sort through the trash until you find the treasure."

"So odds are this is just some junk we've found," I said.

"Odds are," said Tommy. "But we'll find some more piles to investigate. The more hits we get, the more sites we dive, the odds get better."

"So it's a process of elimination," I said. "How many sites did Mel Fisher investigate before he hit paydirt?"

"Thousands," Tommy said. "But we've got different conditions here. The military used the area around the Marquesas for bombing drills. Dummy bombs were all over the place. Old Mel and his boys would drop a marker over whenever they got a hit. They'd come back with divers later. He must have had a thousand markers to investigate. They even found some unexploded ordnance. One day they dropped a marker right on top of the motherlode.

"No bombing drills down here?" I asked.

"Nope," he answered. "And modern shipping stays well away from these reefs and atolls. We know there were some wooden ships that went down somewhere out here. Some that haven't been found."

"How come we didn't drop a marker on our spot?" Bobby asked.

"We start dropping markers we'll have pirates coming out of the woodwork," said Tommy. "The locals ain't much on treasure hunting, but they'll gladly steal whatever someone else finds."

"What happens if they come out to us while I'm under?" asked Holly.

"That's why we need another hand on deck," said Tommy. "A hand with a weapon."

"I'll do it," said Bobby. "I'll stay and help you out."

"What?" I asked. "You're going to stay? What about your boat?"

"I'll worry about that later," he said. "These two have given me the gold bug."

"Just great," I said.

Holly and Tommy looked at me. Bobby looked at me.

"No," I said. "I'm not going on some fool's errand treasure hunt with you."

"You did it for Shirley," Holly said.

"She couldn't do it for herself," I said. "Tommy knows what he's doing. You can take care of yourself. You don't need me tagging along, especially if Bobby is going to stay."

That's when I hoped Holly would try to talk me into staying. I wanted her to at least try to get me to join the hunt. I wanted her to show that she wanted me around. She did no such thing. She just shrugged.

"Suit yourself," she said.

Eleven

We spent another four days searching. We got several more hits. Each time, we circled back for additional passes. More waypoints were entered into the GPS. More sonar images were studied. We got less and less excited with each new discovery. This was just the legwork. The real deal would be the dive operations. There were weather and rough seas to worry about. There was the Mexican Navy and local pirates to watch for. The inevitable mechanical problems would pop up. It would be grueling work. I had no interest in it. After eight days at sea, I was ready to fly back to Florida.

When we got back to Texan Bay, I asked Tommy to settle up with me. I was sure that Sherri would give me a ride to the airport.

"Stick around, Breeze," he said. "I'll pay you in beers for the boat delivery."

"I'd bring it down for you for free," I said. "But I would appreciate airfare home."

"I'll pay you," he said. "Just hoping that you'd reconsider."

"At least someone wants me to stay," I said.

"None of my business," he said. "But I think your girl and Bobby are getting a little chummy."

"I suspect the same," I said. "If so, there's no point in me hanging around."

"Giving up without a fight?" he asked.

"So far, Holly hasn't given me a reason to fight," I said.

"Sorry, bud," he said.

"Yea, me too."

Big Mike was waiting for us when we went to shore. He didn't look happy.

"We had some unwanted visitors while you were gone," he said. "It appears you've brought the gangsters down on us."

"What happened?" I asked.

"A dozen of them showed up," he said. "Overwhelmed us. I got some good licks in but there was too many of them."

"What did they take?"

"Small outboards, binoculars, radios, cash," he said. "Whatever they could grab."

"Anybody hurt?"

"Nothing serious," he said. "But these folks expect to be safe from this crap here. Never had a problem until you had a run-in with them."

"Damn," I said. "I'm real sorry about this. What can we do?"

"You can get on a plane and fly out of here," he said. "You've done enough already."

"What about the thugs?"

"Maybe they've got enough revenge," he said.

"You said yourself that something needed to be done sooner or later," I said.

"Yea, but what?"

"We man up," I said. "Go break some knee caps. Bust some heads."

"We need a small army for that," he said. "Not a lot of muscle here outside of you and me."

"Any healthy young men up in Rio Dulce?"

"There's a few," he said. "I don't know them personally."

"I'll take care of that," I said. "You figure out who else is game here. As soon as we get enough manpower, we'll move on them. I'll fly out as soon as it's over."

I left him to ponder my offer. I thought he might be itching to throw a few punches. I rounded up my crew and we all returned to Tommy's boat. Some of Mike's burgers or barbecue would have been nice, but he wasn't in the mood to entertain us that night.

I spent the next two days poking around the harbor and the marinas in Rio Dulce. Everyone had been a victim of vandalism or knew someone that had been robbed. Most of them were too old to be of much help in a fight, but I managed to recruit four fit men in their forties. I learned that Mike had talked two more guys in his marina to join us. With Mike, Bobby and me, we had nine. We'd be outnumbered, but we had the element of surprise on our side. If we could quickly take out three or four of the bad guys, the numbers would even out.

The gang hung out in an abandoned farmhouse just outside of town. They lived with no electricity or running water. They stole food as well as items they could sell. A cruiser who lost an outboard to thieves could survive, but some of the town folk couldn't afford to have their food stolen. As I listened to the stories of those affected, it became clear that the punks had grown bolder lately. It was time to put a stop to it.

We all met on Big Mike's porch for a strategy session. Our weapons were a baseball bat, assorted lengths of pipe, and an ax handle. We decided to make our raid before dawn. We wanted to catch all of them together at once, with their guard down. We'd sneak up as quietly as we could, then bust in on them.

"This ain't no job for pussies," said Mike. "We catch them sleeping, we whack 'em. Understand? Just run in there and start smacking heads. Let God sort them out later."

I thought that would scare a few of our men off the mission. It did not. Everyone said they were willing to do what had to be done.

"It's for the greater good," Mike said. "In the long run, we'll all be able to live without fear of these thugs."

"It might make future thugs think twice," I added. "Make the place safer for everyone."

"When do we hit them?" asked Bobby. "Tomorrow?"

"Let's all drink tonight," said Mike. "It's on me. Sleep it off tomorrow. You all think long and hard in the meantime. We ride the next night. Meet up here at three in the morning."

Mike and Sherri served up good Texas barbecue and all the beer we could drink. Our little platoon got full and drunk. Mike started telling us stories about the bar room brawls of his younger days. Some of the other guys talked about the last time they'd been in a fight. For the most part, those fights had been decades ago. Holly slipped away, probably to escape the excess testosterone. Bobby didn't talk much. He was busy wrapping pieces of pipe with electrical tape. It made a nice non-slip handle. Tommy partied with us, but he wasn't going along on the raid.

"I'm a runner, not a fighter," he said.

"Done plenty of running myself," I told him. "Sometimes I get backed into a corner, have to fight my way out."

"You feel backed into a corner now?" he asked.

"Mike has evicted me," I explained. "The only reason I'm still here is because of this raid. He blames me for them coming here. Probably blames you too."

"He politely asked me to find a new anchorage," Tommy said.

"What about Holly?" I asked.

"She can stay if she wants," he said. "But she's determined to hunt for gold."

"Maybe it will be safe in Rio Dulce after we take care of business," I said.

"Maybe."

The party broke up around midnight. We found Holly down by the docks, snoozing in a lawn chair.

"I thought you macho fools would be up all night," she said. "Figuring out who had the biggest dick."

"Mike was just getting them pumped up for battle," I said. "Give them some confidence. Get their juices flowing."

"I can't remember ever seeing a more juvenile display," she said. "It's not like you."

"Sometimes peace can only be won through violence," I said. "This is one of those times."

"Violence is never the answer," she said. "Violence is the last refuge of the incompetent. Isaac Asimov."

"People sleep peaceably in their beds at night only because rough men stand ready to do violence on their behalf," I said. "George Orwell."

"I don't like it," she said.

"You don't have to like it," I replied.

The divide between Holly and me grew larger. She didn't speak to me on the way out to the boats. We dropped her off at *Another Adventure*. I thought that Bobby might join her, but he didn't. He probably sensed that she'd had enough manliness for one night.

We went straight for the hammocks. I hung there, wondering if I should confront him. I decided against it. I had nothing against him. I was tired and full of beer. I needed to save my energy for the upcoming raid. I'd fly out of there when it was over. Holly and Bobby could do as they wished without my interference. Maybe Tommy would make them all rich. That would be nice.

We spent the next day keeping our nervous energy in check. Throughout the afternoon, Mike's porch slowly filled up with our soldiers. There was no free beer. There was no barbecue. I bought a burger and a soda. Some of the men wanted booze, but Mike forbid it. We did some more planning. I'd lead half the men through the front door. Mike would lead the rest in through the back. Our instructions were to clobber the first thug we encountered, even if he was asleep. Keep clobbering until there were no more thugs to clobber. We'd drag our hapless victims outside before setting fire to their clubhouse.

Some of the men paced back and forth. One was playing solitaire in the shade of the tiki hut. I relaxed. I wasn't nervous. I was fairly certain we'd win the conflict easily. I'd hit a man in the head before with a pipe. I'd hit a man with a hammer. Those men had been bigger and stronger than I, and certainly bigger and stronger than the punks of Rio Dulce. As long as we executed as planned, it would be over in minutes.

Holly was absent. She stayed on her boat all day. Sherri stayed in the kitchen. She served us burgers and soft drinks without her usual politeness. Tension hung in the air like fog. Just after dark, two big skiffs arrived. Mike had arranged for local captains to run us into Rio Dulce. We loaded our crude weapons and a case of bottled water into each boat. We waited. Some of us napped. Finally, Big Mike rose from his chair and spoke.

"Let's do this," he said. "To the boats, men."

Bobby and the two men from Texan Bay marina were with me. The guys from Rio Dulce rode with Mike. In less than an hour, we made our approach to the town. Our captains idled their skiffs up to the sea wall at the restaurant. We all piled out. They'd disappear and only return on our signal. We stayed quiet and tried to conceal our weapons. The streets were empty and dark. We made the edge of town without incident. We followed a well-beaten trail towards the farm house. The gang had no one on watch. We encountered no trip-wires. We simply walked right up to the edge of the property.

We huddled behind some overgrown bushes. I whispered to the men.

"If anyone wants to back out, now's the time," I said. "No shame in it."

No one responded.

"Nod yes if you're ready," I whispered.

They all nodded yes. I looked at Big Mike.

"Let's go kick some punk ass," he said.

We split off into two groups. Bobby was at my side as we ran to the front door. The place was completely dark. There were no signs of anyone being awake. The door wasn't even locked. I swung the door open and Bobby was the first inside. I saw four young men asleep on the floor. Two of them started to stir when we entered. I took out one and Bobby smacked the other. Our buddies hammered the other two in quick succession.

We heard Big Mike and his men swinging their clubs in another room. Their intended victims had woken when we entered. They still had no defense. I heard the sound of wood against bone. I heard grunts and cries. Eight punks had taken a sharp blow to the head in less than a minute. Where were the rest of them? A flashlight lit up the room.

"Upstairs," yelled Mike.

The stairway was narrow so we had to go single-file. Big Mike led the way. He was met with a wooden chair at the top step. He blocked it with a beefy forearm. It splintered into pieces. Now he was really pissed off. He grabbed the guy and slammed him into a wall. He jammed his big knuckles into the punk's face. I ran past them looking for more. I saw the last of them slip out a window.

"Outside," I said. "They're jumping down."

We all backtracked the way we'd come. My guys went out the front. Mike's guys went out the back. A sweep of the flashlight gave away their position. At least three of them had escaped. They could run, I'll give them that. We had no chance to catch up to them.

"Stop," I said. "Let them run."

"They'd just wait out there until they could jump one of us," said Mike. "It's okay. They'll tell the story for us."

We still had eight thugs in various states of disrepair inside. Some were still unconscious.

Others bled from their head wounds. We carried or prodded them all out into the yard.

"No more thefts," I said. "No vandalism. No harassment. You leave the people alone. Understand?"

"Or we'll be back," said Mike.

One of the guys from Rio Dulce spoke in Spanish. Mike snarled and pointed his ax handle at the man who replied. They understood. There was no further resistance. We'd overwhelmed them and shown a capacity for violent action. This they understood. The point was punctuated when the house went up in flames. We stood and watched it burn. The still unconscious ones were dragged further way from the heat. Those that could walk slowly made their way into the woods.

It was over.

Twelve

Back at the restaurant, Mike gave a loud whistle. Our boat captains appeared out of nowhere. We climbed aboard our respective skiffs. I passed out bottles of water. Mike announced his plans for a party that night. He wanted to celebrate and show his thanks.

"I know it wasn't the battle of the bulge or anything," he said. "But you all showed courage. It's good to know that some men will still stand up when needed."

I kept quiet. I wasn't overly proud of cracking the skull of some dumb kid in a third world country. I just did what had to be done. Bobby, on the other hand, was still full of excitement. He was getting off on the adrenaline. He bragged that his victim was probably still out of it. He said he would have done the same to the ones that got away, given the chance. He'd gotten a taste of blood, and he liked it. The sound of the engine drowned him out once we got underway.

Holly, Tommy, and Sherri were waiting for us at the marina. Sherri immediately noticed the growing lump on Mike's forearm. She pulled him into the kitchen to get some ice to put on it.

"Any other casualties?" asked Tommy.

"That's it," I said. "No one else has a scratch."

"Thank God," said Holly. "You're getting too old to play army."

"Worried about me?" I asked.

"I was worried about all of you," she said. "Bunch of damn fools."

"No sweat," said Bobby. "It went exactly like we planned. We just walked in and busted them up. Nothing to it."

"I don't want to hear about it," said Holly. "I'm glad it's over and everyone is okay."

"Good job, Breeze," said Tommy. "You too, Bobby."

"Mind if I go to the boat and sleep it off?" I asked.

"Go ahead," Tommy said. "I'll hang out here. Sherri says we're having a party later."

"I'm staying here too," said Bobby. "I'm still too pumped to sleep."

Holly gave me a nasty look, like it was my fault that Bobby was acting cocky. Hell, maybe it was. He'd come a long way since leaving Fort Myers Beach.

I plopped down on the musty mattress aboard Tommy's ridiculously rusty boat. I took stock of my situation. I was in Guate-damn-mala and not feeling particularly wanted. Big Mike wanted me gone. Holly had done nothing to indicate that she wanted me to stay. Bobby clearly wanted to take my place. This episode in my life was coming to an end. I'd been the one to bring Holly and Bobby together if that's what was happening. I couldn't muster any enthusiasm for treasure hunting. I'd brought the gang into the lives of Mike's marina residents. How could it have all gone so wrong?

I kept turning it over in my mind. This mission had involved too many working parts. I was on unfamiliar turf, with too many people in my circle. There had been too many outside factors that I couldn't control. I hadn't been able to successfully juggle all of the pieces. I still felt sharp and alert, but maybe I missed something that I should have seen coming. However I added it up, the only answer was to go back home and start over. Keep it simple. Live slow and easy. That's all I ever wanted in the first place.

Something else occurred to me. I had never officially checked into the country. I'd need to check out if I was going to fly. I had a passport, but it had not been stamped upon my entry. I had no official papers. That might be a problem. I'd have to ask Mike about that. I'd go back in for the party, after a nap. I shut down all the thoughts swirling around in my head and drifted off to sleep. Something told me I might need the rest.

When I woke up, I felt fine physically, but the conflicting thoughts and feelings stuck with me. I already felt an empty spot where Holly's essence once lived inside me. Even when we were apart, there had always been the chance that we'd get back together. This was most likely the end for us.

I splashed some water on my face and looked in the mirror. The wrinkles were a bit deeper. The hair was a bit more peppered with gray. Time was working on me. I was fifty-four years old and still wandering around the edges of life. I didn't fit in with polite society, but when I stayed away, loneliness crept in more often than it used to. My dream was simple: a special lady who would go away with me to a tropical island. My dream remained elusive. Time was indeed running out.

I put on a happy face and went back to shore. Folks were starting to gather for the promised party. I found Mike in his usual chair. Ima sat in his lap. I asked about my passport and lack of a visa.

"I forgot about that," he said. "Most of us hire a local pilot. Fly out of that field over behind the hill. He can land you in the Keys or Miami. For the right amount of money."

"What happens when I land?"

"He's got a freight guy. Taxis right into a hangar," he said. "You just walk away."

"Can you arrange it for me?"

"Where to?"

"Marathon?"

"Shouldn't be a problem," he said. "I'll go call him."

Mike was almost eager to assist in my departure. I went to ask Sherri for a beer.

"I understand you're leaving us," she said.

"Whether I wanted to or not," I said.

"It's not personal," she explained. "Mike and I have worked hard to make this place a safe haven for cruisers. It's been our mission for years. We built the tiki. We brought in electricity. Mike wired the docks all by himself. This is our dream. I guess we get a bit defensive if anything happens that threatens it."

"I understand completely," I said. "I just hope you know that I meant no harm."

"Of course not, dear," she said. "You're a victim of circumstances."

"You pay your money and you take your chances," I said. "I'm ready to go home anyway. Thank you for your kind hospitality."

"Good luck to you, Breeze," she said.

I walked around looking for Holly and Bobby. I saw them coming into the dock on Holly's dinghy. It made me flinch. I'd left them on shore earlier. They'd gone out to Holly's boat together while I slept. The three of us joined Tommy at a table in the shade.

"Looks like I'll be saying goodbye soon," I said. "Mike's getting me a plane as we speak."

"I don't know what to say, Breeze," said Holly. "It feels like the end of an era."

"I'd like to talk with you to alone before I go," I said. "If that's okay."

"I think maybe I was trying to avoid that," she said. "You know how I feel about saying goodbye."

"We should be getting good at it by now," I said.

"Never gets easier," she said.

"You two should just forget about each other," Bobby said. "Then you won't have to say goodbye anymore."

His comment really hit me the wrong way. It was an asshole thing to say under the circumstances. I could feel the rage building inside me, but I tamped it down. *Keep your cool, Breeze.* I walked away to get another beer. Bobby was feeling full of himself. If he didn't watch it, I'd have to poke a few holes in his inflated ego. I sat by myself nursing my beer. Something was telling me to stay alert. I trusted my gut in these matters. I scanned everyone in attendance. We weren't exactly friends, but none of them was likely to cause me a problem. I'd led the raid that this party was celebrating, after all. I thought I was square with Big Mike because of that. He was helping me get home. He wouldn't start anything. That left my own people. If I was to have trouble, it would come from Holly, Bobby, or Tommy.

I sought out Tommy, finding him at the bar. He handed me an envelope full of cash.

"Thanks for your help," he said. "Sorry to see you go."

Tommy was no threat. He liked me. We respected each other.

"I want to wish you and your crew the best of luck," I told him. "I'd tell you to look me up if you're ever in Florida, but that doesn't seem likely."

"I won't be going back to Florida," he said. "Easier to hide down here."

"Especially with your millions," I said. "Why do you even want to keep looking for gold?"

"It's what I do," he said. "It's all I know."

"I think I understand," I said.

"We're not that different, you and I," he said. "I'm always looking for that next pile of gold. Your holy grail is a woman you haven't met yet."

"Nothing to do but keep looking," I said.

Big Mike handed me another beer.

"You take off at first light," he said. "You can sleep up here tonight if you want."

"I'll have to go get my stuff," I said. "It's just one bag."

"Either way," he said. "No hard feelings, right?"

"I'm good if you are," I said. "Sorry to have upset things around here."

"It's not even really your fault," he said. "I see that, but I've got a feel for these things. If you stick around, more shit's going to happen."

"I've got a knack for getting into shit," I said.

"Exactly," he said. "Take that shit back to where you came from, and we'll go about our business here."

"I'll be out of your hair in the morning," I said. "Now tell me something honestly. You enjoyed our little invasion, didn't you?"

"I won't confess to enjoyment," he said. "But all my life I've been the peacemaker, and by peacemaker, I mean head knocker. I was worried that age and paradise were making me soft. Nice to know you still got it, if you know what I mean."

"I've been struggling with it myself lately," I admitted. "Starting to notice the signs."

"Don't listen to them," he said. "Go down kicking and screaming."

"I'll just concentrate on going away for now," I said. "Let you get back to normal."

"Nice to have met you, Breeze," he said. "Safe travels."

"Thanks, Mike," I said. "Thanks for everything."

Food was served. Everyone was at least a few drinks in and smiling. I felt better knowing that I would be leaving on good terms with

Mike. I still had that intuition that something was amiss, though. Every time I glanced at Bobby, I caught him looking at me. I wanted to talk to Holly, but he hadn't left her side. I ate light and traded beer for bottled water. Word got around that I was leaving in the morning. Several people came by to wish me well. These were good people, no doubt. They just wanted to enjoy paradise in peace.

I saw Bobby head for the restroom. I made my move.

"Can we talk alone?" I asked Holly. "Just for a few minutes."

"Come on," she said. "Let's go around behind the bar. I don't want anyone to see me if I get all teary-eyed."

We walked together to the backside of the building. When we stopped, Holly gave me a hug.

"I'm so sorry, Breeze," she said.

We held our embrace and looked into each other's eyes. We knew. We were looking for something that we knew we hadn't found in each other.

"I care for you deeply," I said. "I'm sure I always will."

"I feel the same," she said. "But time moves on."

We hugged a little tighter. No tears were shed. Time was moving on.

Bobby burst around the corner. Our moment was over. Bobby Beard wanted to fight. I could see it in his eyes. I didn't want to fight. Holly and I had made our peace. I just wanted to go home. There he stood, ready for a fair fight. I didn't like fair fights much. An old bar brawler once told me to avoid them.

"If you find yourself in a fair fight," he said. "You did something wrong."

My modus operandi had mostly been hitting the other guy with a pipe when he wasn't looking. That chance was long gone. Bobby was ready.

"I think it's about time you got taken down a few notches, old man," he said. "You don't seem so tough anymore. There's a changing of the guard going on."

His neck muscles were tensed. Both of his hands were already clenched into fists. I relaxed my arms and shoulders. *Keep your cool, Breeze.*

"You don't want to do this, Bobby," I said. "It's unnecessary. I'm out of here in the morning."

"That's why it needs to happen now," he said. "I can't let you get away without a proper ass whooping."

"Stop it, Bobby," said Holly. "This is ridiculous."

Time slowed down for me. I studied my opponent. He was almost fifteen years younger than me. He was fit, but he wasn't tough. He may have some gym time, or maybe he played tennis. Somehow, he'd convinced himself that he could take me out. First, we'd had our little encounter with the three punks in Rio Dulce. He'd swung a pipe at a small, sleepy man in an abandoned farmhouse. His inner animal had been released. I may have been getting older, but I was no punk. I didn't want this fight, but if he continued, I'd release my own inner animal. His peacock strutting was pissing me off.

"Just relax, Bobby," I said. "We don't have to do this."

He charged at me like a linebacker about to make a tackle. I stayed relaxed until the last second. My head was clear. Bobby's was not. He'd let his rage overtake his sense. As soon as he reached out to tackle me, I brought a fist up from down low. I planted it squarely on his belly button. He bent over, gasping. I grabbed both ears and pulled his head down sharply until it met my right knee.

It should have been over, but I think I hurt my knee more than his head. He wrestled me to the ground. I really hated wrestling. When you wrestle on the ground in shorts and bare feet, exposed skin tends to suffer. Maybe Bobby had been a wrestler in high school. Before I knew what happened, I was on my hands and knees. Bobby was raining blows to my head from behind. My ears hurt.

"Stop it, Bobby," yelled Holly.

There I was, in the Guatemalan dirt, getting my ears boxed by the man who'd come between me and Holly. I tried to break free, but he had his legs wrapped around me like a boa constrictor. I put my hands up to protect my ears. He flailed away at my hands. The blows weren't devastating, but he didn't seem in any hurry to stop. I had to make him stop. I moved my right hand away from my head.

When the next punch came, I managed to grab his wrist. I tucked it under my shoulder and rolled over on it. I heard things cracking and snapping in his arm. He rolled off of me. His right arm was limp in his lap. The look of anger was gone from his eyes. He was in pain.

That could have been the end of it. He'd lost his will to fight. The pain was unfamiliar to him. He looked confused. It would have been noble of me to walk away. I found myself suddenly lacking in nobility. I let go of my rage. I quit keeping my cool. I released my inner animal.

A quick side kick to the face put him on his back. I was on top of him instantly. I bashed his face with a right, then a left. He tried to shield himself with his good arm. I held it down with one hand and continued punching with the other. Teeth broke. Bones broke. His nose and lips became unrecognizable pieces of bloody flesh.

"Stop it, Breeze," yelled Holly. "You'll kill him."

The animal wanted to kill him. I pounded away, punishing him for his transgressions. I wanted to beat the youth and ego out of him.

I wanted to make him pay for trying to replace me.

"I don't look so old now, do I motherfucker?" I yelled.

He was everything I no longer was, and I hated him for it. Someday, he might be man enough to take me out, but today was not that day. Holly tried to pull me off. I saw terror in her eyes when I pushed her out of the way.

"Please stop," she said. "Please, Breeze. Stop."

She was crying. I was oblivious. I only felt rage. The rage fed the animal. I kept beating poor Bobby Beard long after he lost consciousness.

It was Big Mike that stopped me. He lifted me in the air and held me in a bear hug so tight I couldn't breathe. My feet dangled a foot off the ground. I didn't resist. He could crush me if he wanted to. This latest development didn't make him any happier about my presence. He carried me past the bar and the curious onlookers. He carried me down the walkway to the docks. I was seriously short of breath. He plopped me down on a bench and put his meaty finger in my face.

"You sit right there, you son of a bitch," he said. "Let me get to the bottom of this. Don't move until I get back."

I watched him walk back to the bar. I took in some deep breaths. I was in deep shit with him now. I could only hope to survive until the morning.

My hands were covered in blood. Most of it was Bobby's. I didn't dare go wash them off. I just sat and waited. Tommy came down and sat next to me.

"Jesus, Breeze," he said.

"Sit with me," I said. "If Mike doesn't kill me, I'll need a ride to the boat."

Tommy stayed with me. He filled a bucket with water and helped me clean up. I had blood on my shirt, my face, and my hair. My knuckles were swelling quickly. I saw Mike carry Bobby's lifeless body inside. Holly and Sherri hovered over him.

Eventually, Mike came for me. He was shaking his head back and forth. I was unsure of his verdict.

"I talked with Holly," he said. "She says you tried to avoid the fight. That it was Bobby who caused it."

"I didn't start it," I said.

"You damn sure finished it," he said. "Now here's the problem. She says that you kept pounding him long after you'd won the fight."

"That's true," I said. "I can't deny it."

"Why would you go and do that?" he asked. "He's in bad shape, Breeze. You damned near beat him to death."

"He challenged me," I said. "If things would have gone the other way, you can bet he'd have done the same."

"I'm not so sure," he said. "It takes a certain kind of man to lay down a beating like that. Bobby doesn't have it in him."

"I just wanted to go home," I said. "Bobby pushed me. I didn't want to fight. What happened to him after that is his fault."

"Looks like he didn't know what he was getting into," he said. "I'll be glad when you're gone from here. Your fault or not, trouble follows you."

"Am I free to go?"

"If he's still alive in the morning," he said. "I'll let you get on that plane. If he doesn't make it, we'll have to call the law."

"It's that bad?" I asked.

"It's that bad," he said. "You might want to pray for him tonight."

"Shit," I said. "Can you get him to the hospital?"

"Afraid to move him," he said. "We got a doctor on the way."

"I hope he makes it," I said.

"You better hope," he said. "And pray."

Thirteen

Tommy took me out to his boat. My brain was in a fog. My hands had blown up like beach balls. My ears still stung. If Bobby died, Mike would turn me over to the law. I was sick about what I had done. I'd lost my cool. I'd never been so vicious in my life. I rushed to the rail and threw up over the side. The animal had retreated to his lair. Now I was just Breeze. I was afraid. I was afraid that Bobby would die. I was afraid that I'd spend the rest of my life in a Guatemalan jail. I was appalled at what I'd done. There was no way to justify my actions.

The only time I'd ever snapped like that was when my wife died, but that hadn't been my fault. The actions that I took afterward were cold and calculated. This time I had acted with wild abandon. I'd become a savage. Something about Bobby had made me into a monster, however briefly. I just couldn't wrap my brain around it. Holly had seen it all happen. She was terrified. There was nothing I could say to her that would make any sense.

I choked down a few ounces of rum to calm me down. It burned in my recently evacuated belly. I cooled it off with a beer.

"What am I going to do?" I said aloud.

"If it was me," Tommy said. "I'd slip past the marina tonight and be waiting when the plane lands."

"Mike knows the plane is coming at first light," I said.

"He thinks you'll dinghy into the marina in the morning," he said. "You'll want to know if Bobby made it or not."

"So just pop out of the bushes and flag down the pilot?" I asked.

"Wave some cash at him and tell him to take off," he said. "All these bush pilots are the same. It's all about the cash. He's probably happy it ain't drugs this time."

"Might work," I said.

"You got any better ideas?"

"I can't even think right now," I said. "But my first instinct is to run."

"Mine too," he said. "I'll drop you off over to the east of the marina a few hours before sunrise. Sneak around the perimeter until you hit the trail that runs to the meadow."

"What about you?" I asked. "Mike will realize that you helped me escape."

"I'm leaving anyway," he said. "I won't tell you where I'm tying up next. That way you can't tell anyone else if you get nabbed."

"Will you be in touch with Holly?" I asked.

"That was the plan before tonight," he said. "You took out my other deckhand."

"Yeah, sorry about that," I said.

"I trust you, Breeze," he said. "But if you get caught up with the law, either here or back in Florida, you can't tell them where I am or even where I've been. You got it? You know nothing."

"Got it," I said. "Tommy who?"

"I've got a guy in Guatemala City working on a new identity for me," he said. "Once I put you on the beach, we won't see each other again."

I tried to shake his hand but mine was swollen beyond use. I gave him a half-ass man hug instead. I lay down for a few hours. Surprisingly, I fell into a deep sleep.

Tommy woke me at four in the morning. I grabbed my bag and tossed it in the dinghy. We headed east first, then turned back towards the shoreline beyond the marina. As soon as the bow hit the sand I was out and into the mangroves. There were no further goodbyes exchanged. I picked my way through the muck close to shore until I made dry land. The flora surrounding the marina was mostly overgrown and thick. I crawled when I had to. Eventually, I found the trail and jogged up over the hill and down into the meadow. It didn't look like much of a landing strip. I hoped the pilot knew what he was doing.

I crossed over to the other side, noting how some of the grass had been knocked down. A plane had landed here recently. There was no wreckage, so I guessed he made it in and back out. I crouched down at the edge of the woods, making myself as small as possible. I waited.

The sun had not risen yet, but the sky was starting to lighten. I heard the plane before I saw it. The pilot steered it in just over the tree tops. He dropped like a rock towards the grass and pulled up at the last possible instant. His wheels hit hard. He bounced twice before braking hard. He came to a stop with plenty of room to spare. I broke cover and sprinted towards the plane.

He was just starting to open the door when I showed up, cash in hand.

"Let's take her back up," I said. "Right now."

"I thought Mike might want to say hi," he said.

"No time for that," I said. "I'll double the fare. Let's go right now."

"It's your money," he said. "My name's Matt. Matt Lehn."

"Nice to meet you," I said. "Now get us out of here."

I didn't tell him my name. I didn't talk much at all. Matt did all of the talking. We went down the makeshift runway and made a U-turn. I thought we'd crash into the trees before gaining enough altitude, but we shot up at a crazy angle and missed the trees. I looked down and saw Big Mike coming down the hill towards the meadow. He was too late. We were airborne.

"Weather is good. Winds are light," said Matt. "Should be an easy flight."

"You do this a lot?" I asked.

"Twice a month to Marathon," he said. "Twice to Miami. It's usually freight, not people."

"Pay good?"

"Better than selling insurance did," he said. "Had my own agency. Nice house with a pool. One day I couldn't take it anymore. I sold it all after I got my pilot's license. Took off and never looked back."

"So you're an expat," I said.

"Expat, ex-marine, ex-husband," he said. "Left it all behind."

He still wore his hair with a military cut. His aviator sunglasses reflected the sun as we flew just above the Caribbean Sea. He seemed to be enjoying the flight.

"So who'd you beat up?" he asked, pointing at my hands.

"I'd rather not discuss it," I said. "I'd like to forget it ever happened."

"No problem," he said. "I'm very good at forgetting who or what has been on my plane."

"Good," I said. "I was never here."

"Don't even know your name," he said.

"We'll just keep it that way, if you don't mind," I said.

I napped for the rest of the flight. Matt nudged me before calling the tower at Marathon airport. We came down over the harbor. I could see *Leap of Faith* floating on her mooring. Matt landed his plane like a professional on the smooth tarmac. He stayed powered up and taxied to an open hangar. As soon as we entered, the doors were pulled closed behind us. He shut down the engine.

"That door there leads to some offices," he said. "Just follow the exit signs out of the building."

I paid him twice the agreed upon fee. He didn't argue. He took the cash and smiled at me.

"Good luck, amigo," he said.

"Thanks, man," I said.

I walked out into the afternoon sun. If I had a phone, I could get a cab to the dinghy dock for five bucks. I didn't have a phone. The walk was a hot and sweaty one. I was dying of thirst by the time I got to the Lobster House. It was still happy hour. I slammed three beers while sitting in the air-conditioned bar. The cool refreshment perked me up enough to walk the rest of the way.

My dinghy was right where I'd left it. It was still inflated, but full of water. I used a cut up bleach bottle to bail it out. The motor started on the second pull. Things weren't going too badly. Maybe I'd make it out of this. I was happy to finally be back with *Miss Leap*. She smelled like mildew and bilge. She needed my attention, but first, I needed rest.

I poured some rum over ice and sat on the back deck. I tried to relax. I tried to figure out how things went so wrong. It seemed like I'd just left Fort Myers Beach a few days ago. I'd made love to Jennifer and taken Bobby on a great adventure. All was right with my world back then. Now it had all turned to shit. I was disgusted with myself.

I chugged down the rest of the rum and went to bed. My sheets and pillow case smelled liked mildew. I smelled like sweat and fear. I was too defeated and too tired to care. I'd shrunk my world down to just me and my boat. As long as I had *Miss Leap*, I could make it. I'd ride her out of this place. We'd go somewhere quiet and recover. I'd clean her up. I'd clean myself up. Life would go on. Just before passing out, I said a silent prayer for Bobby.

I woke up with the sunrise. I'd been out for twelve hours straight. The swelling in my knuckles had come down, but they still ached. I was confused. It took me a few minutes to realize that I was in Marathon. I started to replay the events of the past few days in my mind but stopped before my fight with Bobby. I turned my concentration to my present situation. How much fuel did I have? How much water was in the tanks? I checked my freezer and pantry for food. I checked the oil and coolant levels. I had enough of everything except clean clothes. I loathed the idea of using Boot Key's laundry room. I didn't want to be around people. I threw a couple shirts and two pairs of shorts into a bucket of water with a shot of detergent. I fired up the engine and listened to her purr.

All I wanted to do was run. I had a burning desire to leave that place. Everything else could be taken care of later. I wanted to put as many miles as I could between me and the trouble I'd left behind. I decided that the Everglades would hide me pretty damn well if someone was looking for me. I set a course for Little Shark River. I had a love-hate relationship with that place. It was beautiful. It was primitive. It harbored man-eating mosquitoes that I feared more than the gators.

It took seven hours to make the mouth of the river. I usually anchored just inside, but this time I went as far upriver as I could go. I dropped anchor in the dark mud and deployed the bug screens. I spent the rest of the daylight hours wiping down the interior walls of my boat, which then smelled like vinegar for a few days. I rinsed my sheets as best I could and hung them up to dry on the bridge. I stayed busy in an attempt to keep the demons at bay. I used way too much water for a shower. I wanted to wash it all away. It was my first good shower in a long time. The loss of water would shorten my stay. Sooner or later I'd have to go to civilization to refill the tanks. I rinsed my soapy clothes in the shower water. I hung them up next to the sheets.

I fixed a decent meal after sunset. I couldn't sit outside after dark. The bugs were horrendous. I watched them cover the screens. They smelled blood and tried in vain to get inside. As soon as it cooled off enough, I closed all the windows, just in case they found a hole in my defense. I sat in silence. I told myself that this would blow over. I could go back to Pelican Bay and put myself back together. No one was looking for me. If they were, they'd have a hard time finding me in Little Shark.

I spent my days fishing from the dinghy. Tarpon swam all over the place, but they were inedible. I found some good-sized speckled trout around a little island. I ate trout every night until I was sick of them. After that, I ventured up the natural canals and pulled some snook out of the mangroves. I wasn't sure if they were in season, or what the size limit was, but I didn't care. Abiding by the fishery laws wasn't high on my list of priorities. I supplemented my fish diet with canned vegetables. There was no safe place to go to land, no beach to walk on. I really didn't want to risk swimming. There were too many gators around.

After a few weeks, my world started feeling really small. I loved my boat. It was plenty big for just me, but I really yearned to step foot on solid land and walk around. Eventually, I ran out of rum, which was no big deal. I only had enough water left to last a few more days. I was almost out of bug spray too, which was a big deal. There weren't too many hardy souls that could last in the Everglades for weeks. They certainly couldn't do it without bug spray. I was forced to figure out my next step.

Getting water meant rejoining civilization. If I was going to do that, I preferred Fort Myers Beach, which was too far to make in one day. I decided to head for Marco Island first. Instead of my normal anchorage in Factory Bay, I'd hide way back in Smokehouse Bay. There was a grocery store near there. I couldn't take on water, but I could buy bottled water to hold me over. Maybe I could find some rum too.

I said goodbye to my bug-infested gator haven and pulled up my anchor. I pointed *Leap of Faith* towards the Gulf and motored away from safety. The run to Marco took nine hours. I crept through the tricky channel of Collier Creek until it opened up into Smokehouse Bay. My first order of business was to go to land. I loaded up the dinghy with cases of bottled water, cases of beer, and some fresh meat. After putting away my groceries, I returned to land in search of a liquor store. I bought all the rum I could carry.

As I went back and forth, I observed the people I encountered. I was invisible to them. No one here knew who I was or what I had done. It looked like I'd be okay here if I chose to stay. That changed quickly. Soon after returning to my boat, I was paid a visit by the Sheriff's Department. The officer asked to come along side. I didn't think it would be wise to say no.

"What can I help you with?" I asked.

"Just a friendly welcome," he said. "How long you figure you'll stay here?"

"I just got here today," I said. "I hadn't really decided yet."

"The folks in these houses back here would prefer you limit your visit to three days at the most," he told me.

"Is that some kind of rule?" I asked.

"Technically no," he said. "I can't really run you off, but they'll start calling me if you stay too long. I'll have to come out and give you friendly reminders every time they do."

"I think I get the gist," I said. "Don't want to stay where I'm not welcome. I'll move on tomorrow."

"Safe travels," he said.

"Thank you, officer," I said.

The last thing I needed was a visit from the cops every day. I had no clue if anyone was looking for me, but if there was any sort of bulletin about me, sooner or later the local cops would figure it out. It looked like I was continuing to Fort Myers Beach after all. I desperately needed to fill my water tanks. They had free, clean water right at the dinghy dock. The Upper Deck was also right next to the dinghy dock. I could picture Jennifer handing me a cold beer. I could see her smile. I was beginning to think I should have never left Fort Myers Beach in the first place. I could have skipped all the excitement in Guatemala.

The reason I had left was to find Holly. I couldn't have foreseen what happened after that. I really thought that she and I might give it another go. Things didn't work out that way. I certainly couldn't have known that I'd end up in Central America on a rusty old shrimper. How did things spin out of control so often? I really needed to think that through.

I was a smart enough guy. I was alert and constantly aware of my surroundings. I could judge people. I was rational in my thinking most of the time. What was I doing wrong? I'd found myself up to my asshole in alligators too many times. It was time to stay out of the swamp. Wanderlust was the problem. I was really alive when I had someplace to go, and a reason to get there. Having a clear cut mission was my drug. I could settle down for months at a time when necessary, but the urge to move always caught up to me sooner or later. I jumped at every chance that presented itself. That's how I always ended up in trouble. I needed to learn to say no to those adventures. I wasn't sure I could do that, but at least I recognized the problem.

On the way up the coast, I couldn't stop thinking about Bobby. Something happened to him down there. Being like me wasn't enough for him. He had to take over. He was the young buck challenging the old leader. He'd grown up on the trip. He'd grown so much that he thought he needed to defeat me to prove himself. He wanted Holly, and I was a deterrent to that. If he could show me up, I would no longer be a threat. He had convinced himself that he was ready to take over.

He had pushed me into a corner, leaving me no options. It was a tragic mistake on his part. I felt no guilt about winning. Hell, I was proud of myself. Winning beat the alternative. I was not proud of turning his face to mush. I was not proud of losing my humanity, no matter how briefly. The look of terror in Holly's eyes haunted me. Did Bobby make it?

I spent most of the trip replaying that confrontation in my mind. I couldn't recover whatever it was that made me lose control. All I could think was that Bobby had the nerve to challenge me, and I couldn't tolerate that. He had no right to think he could replace me. Or was it just about Holly? I wasn't even sure if the two of them were lovers, but I hated the prospect. I unleashed that hatred on Bobby Beard, maybe killing him in the process. That was a very bad thing. I normally had a pretty high opinion of myself, but that had changed. I'd seen the demon inside, and he wasn't a very nice fellow. I never wanted to see him again.

I was in a sour mood by the time I arrived at my destination. After grabbing a mooring ball, I quickly headed for the showers. I hadn't been really clean for a couple of weeks. The showers that the mooring field provided were the best I'd found for boaters anywhere. They were large tiled spaces, with plenty of hot water and plenty of pressure. I made it as hot as I could stand. I stood there and let that steamy spray pound my skin. It was the best shower I ever had. It not only washed away the dirt, it helped me recover from my funk. I felt great afterward.

The next logical step was to climb the stairs to the Upper Deck and see Jennifer again. I hesitated. When we'd last parted, she'd made herself clear. She'd satisfied her curiosity. We'd never be a couple, though. What if I wanted to stay here with her? Would she see me then?

Who was I kidding? I was never going to stay nailed down in Fort Myers Beach. I decided to get my head straight before talking to her. I threw my shower bag in the dinghy and retreated to my boat. I sat on the back deck with a beer in hand. I could see Diver Dan's boat up the river. There was a hole where One-legged Beth's boat had been. Robin's boat was hidden behind some mangroves. I hoped that Beth was doing well in her new surroundings. I wondered if Dan had heard from her, or if she was gone forever.

I drank one beer after another. I drank until the sharp edges of my anguish got a little fuzzy. Then I drank some more. I was tired of thinking about Bobby. I was tired of thinking about Holly. I drowned both of them in booze until the thinking stopped. I passed out in my deck chair.

Fourteen

Sometime later that night, the mangrove mob showed up. The bums that had used Beth discovered my presence and sought their revenge. I was stupid drunk, never heard them coming. I didn't wake up until they were standing over me. Realizing their advantage, they started pummeling me, right there in my chair. Even drunk, I probably could have held my own against them, but I didn't fight back. I let them beat me. I deserved it, I told myself. It didn't hurt that much. The booze had made me numb. My lack of resistance took all of the fun out of it for them. They quickly tired of it. They called me some names and left. Maybe now they were satisfied. Maybe I wouldn't have to worry about them anymore. They sure showed me.

When I woke up the next morning, the booze was no longer masking the pain. I had a fat lip and a busted up nose. One eye was swollen. There was blood on my shirt and crusted blood in my mustache. I was a mess. Dried blood stained my sheets and pillow. I probably should have cleaned up before going to bed, but I didn't even remember going to bed. I turned on the coffee maker and ate a handful of Advil. Letting those bums use me for a punching bag had been a really bad idea.

The sour mood came back, accompanied by a sore face. No amount of showering was going to fix it this time. I couldn't let Jennifer see me like this. It wasn't vanity, it was my pride. How was I going to explain it? I let three bums work me over because I felt so bad about what I did to Bobby? I was a winner. Winners didn't get beat up by bums. Jennifer would have to wait until I looked more presentable.

I went to the sink to wash my face. The faucet sputtered briefly then quit. I was out of water. My day was only getting worse. I used a wash rag and bottled water to get the blood off of my face. I put my shirt and the sheets into the pillow case. It made a nice laundry bag. I loaded my jerry cans into the dinghy and made my way to the dock. I filled the jugs and returned to the boat. I dumped the cans into my water tanks. I repeated the process until my tanks were full. I was sweaty and hungry.

Bonita Bills was still serving breakfast. They didn't care if I was sweaty and dirty. I rode over and tied up to their dock. I found Diver Dan inside drinking coffee.

"What happened to you?" he asked.

"You should have seen the other guy," I told him. "How're things in the back-water?"

"It's been quiet," he said. "Peaceful even."

"Heard from Beth?"

"She calls," he said. "Says she's clean. Says she likes it up there."

"Good to hear," I said.

"I suppose you want me to thank you for helping her out," he said.

"Not necessary," I said.

"You done a good deed," he said. "You and that Bobby fellow. I go back and forth on the consequences."

"How's that?"

"Because now she's gone," he said. "It's peaceful, but sometimes a bit lonely."

"We had to get her out of here," I said. "You can always go up there and visit."

"On the other hand," he said. "Sometimes I think it's better to let her stay gone."

"You'll have to work that one out on your own," I said.

"Yup."

"Good seeing you, Dan," I said. "I'm going to go hide someplace for a while. I'll be back, though."

"Until the heat is off?" he asked. "What have you gotten into now?"

"Until my face returns to its somewhat normal appearance," I said.

"Somebody kicked the tar out of you," he said. "That's for sure."

"Give it a couple of weeks," I said. "I'll look you up when I get back."

After breakfast, I went straight back to the boat. I had full water tanks. I had groceries, beer, and booze. I could think of no reason to stick around. It was only a five hour trip to Pelican Bay. I fired up the engine, pulled up the anchor, and started heading north. The Upper Deck was to my port side as I passed under the bridge. If Jennifer was working, she probably saw me leaving. If she was up there watching, I'd left her wondering why I hadn't stopped in.

Once I cleared the markers, I steered towards the lighthouse at the bottom of Sanibel Island. I veered back east and went under the causeway. I joined the ICW near St. James City. I was once again back in my home waters. They weren't as pretty as the Bahamas or even the Keys, but they were comfortable to me. *Miss Leap* had made this trip dozens of times. We entered Pine Island Sound. Captiva was to my west. The old stilt fishing houses were to my east. We passed Cabbage Key and Useppa. I turned off the ICW at marker seventy-four and made my approach to Pelican Pass.

The sand bar at the entrance had shifted since I'd been there last. Half of it was gone. The sand that had washed away had been deposited into the channel. I slowed. I could see the white sand from my vantage point on the bridge. I scooted to port about fifty feet to find the deep water. I maintained my slow speed as I angled towards the park service docks. The ferries that ran from Punta Gorda had deep drafts. I knew they'd keep the channel open with their daily back and forth trips.

The water deepened beyond the docks. I motored south of Manatee Cove. I settled in my usual spot and dropped the hook. After rigging a bridle to the anchor chain, I backed down until the anchor was firmly dug in. I was home. I would heal. I always did. There was something therapeutic about Pelican Bay and Cayo Costa. This time, I not only had wounds of the flesh, I had wounds to my heart and soul. There was virtually no chance that I'd ever see Holly again. I didn't know if Bobby was dead or alive. My hands were better, but now my face was battered.

I'd sent Beth away for her own good. Dan didn't know if he was grateful to me or not. Jimi D's whereabouts were unknown. Holly was in Guatemala looking for gold. Other than Jennifer, I'd managed to run off every friend I had. I wasn't even sure that she would want to see me again. It looked like I'd be doing without friends for the time being. It was just as well. I needed some alone time to sort things out.

I had frozen two wet washcloths. I took them out of the freezer and laid them over my face. I sat on the back deck and let the sun start to thaw them out. Cold water trickled down my face and onto my neck. It felt good. Later I took stock in the mirror. The swollen eye had turned purple. The cut on my nose might leave a scar. I was happy that those bums weren't a tougher bunch. If better men had caught me with my guard down like that, it would have been disastrous. Staying alert was a full-time job, and I had been slacking. I need to stay closer to sober at all times. I needed to come to terms with myself so that I could keep a clear head. If age was slowing me down, then I needed to try even harder.

After dinner, I allowed myself two beers to wash down the sunset. There were two other boats in the bay, but I'd anchored far from them. I kept putting my wet washcloths back in the freezer after they thawed. Before going to bed, I applied an anti-bacterial cream to my cuts. Lying in my bunk, I could hear the familiar sounds of my home. An osprey chirped from his perch on the island. Dolphins surfaced to breathe. There was a slight lapping of water on the hull. It was all music to me. I slept deeply. No dreams interrupted me. I slept long and hard, only waking when the sun reached my eyes through the port light.

It had been a restorative sleep. I was too exhausted to think about all the problems that were bothering me. My improvised ice packs had brought down the swelling in my face. I was encouraged by the rest and the physical improvement. I'd gone twelve hours without worrying, so I decided to continue not worrying. Those problems seemed much farther away. I vowed to ignore them. I'd just put them out of my mind and keep on keeping on.

I ate breakfast with one hand and held a washcloth on my face with the other. As soon as I was finished, I took the dinghy to the beach. I walked a couple miles south at a brisk pace. On the way back, I moved slower. I inspected the shells and sand dollars along the way. I rested for a bit, then took a short swim. The salt water stung my cuts and abrasions. I floated out there in the Gulf of Mexico. I was going to be okay. I still had this life. I still had my boat and this beach. I had no job to report to. I had no boss to tell me what to do. I had my own little piece of paradise. In spite of how everything had gone so wrong, at that moment I was grateful.

I carried my gratitude back to *Leap of Faith*. I noticed her water line was getting a little furry. Some of the teak needed a maintenance coat. I sat down and made a list of chores that would keep me busy for a few weeks. Instead of starting work on the list, I went fishing. I caught dinner first, then took a nap. I remembered why I loved this lifestyle so much.

My daily walks got longer. Soon they turned into jogs. I swam longer too. I scrubbed the hull and shined the teak trim. I tightened screws and waxed fiberglass. I either worked or worked out, all day long. I ate well. I maintained my two beer per day ration. I hid the rum down in the bilge so I wouldn't have to look at it. My old boat appreciated the attention. So did my body. My face healed nicely. I just had the faint trace of a scar on my nose. It added character. I felt healthy and strong. I was enjoying the time alone. I rarely thought about Holly or Bobby. I did think about Jennifer. I was moving on. I needed to move on.

Pelican Bay was working its magic. I enjoyed the good weather and the nightly sunsets. I recognized the same dolphin every morning after sunrise. He had a distinctive cut in his dorsal fin. I named him Notch. Other boats came and went. No one bothered me. I didn't bother them. Two weeks passed and I made no effort to return to Fort Myers Beach. After the third week, I knew I'd have to go back eventually. In order to conserve water, I took saltwater baths. I rinsed lightly with my precious fresh water. Occasionally, I'd walk across the island and use the outdoor showers at the campground.

My water and supplies lasted a month. I was in good shape, both physically and mentally. My head was clear. I honed my sense of awareness, noticing every small detail of my surroundings wherever I went. Whenever a new boat arrived, I'd watch them. Are they cruisers or weekenders? How old are they? Are they husband and wife, or boyfriend and girlfriend? Do they have any skills, or are they credit card captains? I was prepared to go back, but I was in no hurry. Finally, the lack of water forced me to go back. I hadn't spoken to another soul for a month. It would feel strange to rejoin society. I didn't belong there.

I made the run back down to Fort Myers Beach once the water tanks were completely empty. When I entered the mooring field, I scanned the boats. There were a few newcomers in the field. I kept an eye out for bums in skiffs. I secured the boat to a ball and shut the engine down. The shrimp fleet was out of town, working the Gulf between Florida and Texas. I was low on food, so I decided to eat at the Upper Deck and check in on Jennifer. I got a shower on land and put on my best shirt.

I climbed the steps to the bar and saw Jennifer. I took an open stool in the middle of the bar.

"What can I get you?" she said.

There was no friendly greeting, no questions about where I'd been or how I was doing. She treated me like a complete stranger. She kept flicking her eyes about, first to the left, then to the right. She pointed with her shoulder. I didn't know what she was trying to tell me. I shrugged. She wrote something on a napkin and slid it over to me.

Boyfriend. Left. Blue shirt. FBI. Right. White shirt.

Boyfriend? FBI? What had I walked into?

The only white shirt in the bar was worn by a woman. She was moderately attractive, but her dark brown hair was too short for my tastes. She was on the thin side but had curves in the right places. She was focused on the television. I took a glance at the boyfriend. He was a good looking guy, younger than me. He was eating a pizza that looked really good. I looked back at the woman. She smiled at me. All sorts of alarms were going off in my head, mostly because of three little letters. FBI. I thought I was finished with them. I'd been cleared. They weren't supposed to be looking for me. I thought about getting up and exiting down the stairs. Jennifer gave me a panicked look.

Before I could decide, the woman approached me.

"Meade Breeze?" she asked.

"Depends on who's asking," I said.

"Agent Brody," she said, showing me her badge.

"To what do I owe the pleasure?" I asked.

"Mind if I sit?" she asked.

"Help yourself."

She motioned for another drink. I watched Jennifer mix a rum and coke.

"You always drink on the job?" I asked.

"I'm off duty," she said. "Actually, I'm kind of on a sabbatical."

"Then why are you stalking me?" I said. "I've done nothing wrong."

"Maybe, maybe not," she said. "I just had a personal interest in finding you."

"Why is that?"

"The FBI was looking for you because of the Taylor Ford incident," she said. "I was on the case."

"And you didn't find me," I said. "And then I was cleared."

"Correct," she said. "But it bothered me that we couldn't find you."

"How so?"

"All of the tools that we normally use to track someone down didn't apply to you," she said. "Cell phones, credit cards, ATM machines, license plate readers, computers. You are a ghost."

"But here you sit," I said. "Care to tell my why you returned to the search? Maybe how you found me?"

"I have to admit something," she said. "I was intrigued by you. It didn't occur to us that someone could survive without a phone or at least a debit card. We were baffled that we came up empty. You don't even have a current driver's license."

"So you're not here on official business?" I asked. "I'm not a wanted man?"

"I'll get to that," she said.

"It's a pretty important detail," I said. "Don't keep me in suspense."

"Let me answer your other question first," she said. "I found you with good old-fashioned gumshoe detective work. Or boat shoe in this case."

"You came here by boat?"

"That's right," she said. "We knew that you were on a boat. I figured I'd need one to find you. According to the U.S. Coast Guard, your vessel was built in Taiwan in 1980. It is thirty-six feet long. A slow trawler. According to

Boat US, it's powered by a single engine, 120 horsepower diesel. You've been towed only once, from somewhere near Cape Sable to Marathon. You had extensive repairs done at the Marathon Boatyard."

"You've been doing your homework," I said. "Why am I that important?"

"Everyone leaves a trace," she said. "Yours was just harder to find. I made it my mission to find you."

"Why? How?"

"I wanted to meet the man who evaded the FBI, who evaded me," she said. "I needed to prove that I could track you down."

"Congratulations, I guess."

"We knew that Fort Myers Beach was one of the places you frequented," she said. "I got myself a boat and moved in. I asked around. Either no one knows you, or they wouldn't talk. I suspect you have some loyal friends. Jennifer here wouldn't answer my questions either, but I determined that she was being evasive. This is the closest bar to the dinghy dock. I was pretty sure that you'd been here and that she knows you."

"What if I never showed up?"

"My next stop was Pelican Bay," she said. "After that Punta Gorda."

"All of this is on your own time?"

"Yes, but I'm still in touch," she said. "There have been quite a few new developments recently."

"Related to me?"

"Unfortunately yes," she said. "We knew that you left here with another man by the name of Bobby Beard. We have all the information on his boat, but it hasn't turned up. The man himself, though, has been located."

The sound of Bobby Beard's name was like a slap in the face. I'd been suppressing any memory of him. This chick had dug deeper than I could have ever imagined. I tried to stay cool.

"How'd you find him?"

"The curious thing was where we found him," she said. "In a hospital in Guatemala City. When he was first brought in, the hospital contacted the American embassy there. Bingo, we found Bobby Beard."

"Your tentacles reach pretty far," I said.

"Trust me," she said. "If you knew the half of it, you'd be glad you don't have a phone or any other electronic device."

"How's he doing?" I asked.

"He's in a coma," she said. "He's not talking, but the staff is. So are the people at a little place called Texan Bay. We learned that he was brought in from the marina there. The owners were more than happy to cooperate. You didn't make any friends there."

"It was a matter of self-defense," I said.

"Maybe so," she said. "But if he dies there could still be a manslaughter charge."

"Am I under arrest?"

"Not yet," she said. "But that possibility is hanging over you. I'll keep an eye on you in the meantime."

"At what point does this go from personal to professional?" I asked. "And at what point is your surveillance an illegal act? I must have some legal protections here."

"Feel free to consult with a lawyer," she said. "You might want to find one who's familiar with international laws that relate to extradition, and the powers granted my agency in these matters."

She excused herself to use the restroom. I watched her walk. She came across as stern and professional. Her walk betrayed her femininity. I still didn't like the hair. It barely came down to her ears, with bangs that hung down in front of her eyes. I couldn't understand why she had put so much time and energy into locating me. She'd bought a boat for crying out loud. I'd have to figure out a way to shake her, no matter how nice her body was. She was a cop. I bet that she couldn't last a week living on the hook. She might be tough for a woman, but the heat and the bugs would drive her to retreat to the life she was about to leave behind.

She smiled when she returned. She didn't have the face of a classic beauty, but she did have a nice smile. It took the edge off her seriousness.

"So you're going to just follow me around," I asked.

"You could make it easy on me," she said. "Just stay here until the matter is resolved."

"We can meet here and drink together every night," I said.

"I'd prefer you didn't," Jennifer said. "For a couple reasons."

"You serious with this guy?" I asked.

"He's perfect," she said. "Please don't screw it up for me."

"I wish you nothing but happiness," I said.

"I knew that you two were friends," said Brody.

Fifteen

It occurred to me that I may have inadvertently led Brody to Tommy's hideout. She hadn't mentioned him, or Holly, so I didn't say anything about it. I didn't even know if she knew who Tommy was. She could have spoken to him and never realized that he was a fugitive. Hopefully, Tommy and Holly had moved on before anyone from the FBI came poking around.

"Let's move to a table," I said. "Order a pizza. I don't want to distract Jennifer with my drama."

Jennifer rolled her eyes. Her boyfriend looked on quizzically. She introduced him as Jason. Brody and I moved to a table in the back, away from the bar.

"I assumed you focused on this part of Florida based on what Taylor told you," I said.

"She said you met in Punta Gorda," she replied. "And that you took her to Pelican Bay and Fort Myers Beach. When you needed to come to shore, you came here or went to Punta Gorda. Sometimes you stayed at Laishley Park Marina."

"Sometimes I stay gone for many months at a time," I said. "You got lucky catching me here."

"You make your own luck, sometimes," she said. "Technology didn't work, but human interaction certainly helped."

"Seems like an inefficient use of resources," I said. "I can't be that important to the FBI."

"It became important to me," she said. "You popped up on our radar several times. A shooting in Miami. Another shooting in the Bahamas. A fugitive apprehension by a private citizen in Texas. I replayed the news stories about that one. I got my first look at you. I thought you were a handsome man."

"Still think I'm handsome in person?" I asked.

"A little rougher around the edges than I expected," she said. "But I can see where women would fall for you. You've obviously lived an exciting life."

"I'm actually quite boring," I said. "I just sit on my boat, drink beer and watch the sunset."

"Sounds enchanting," she said. "But you apparently get around. I bet you've seen some things in your travels."

"I feel like I'm talking to my own personal historian," I said. "You know so much about me."

"I don't know what makes you tick," she said. "I'm curious."

"My disdain for modern society makes me want to live alone in the wilderness," I said. "But, that human interaction thing you mentioned keeps bringing me back. That, and the need for food and water."

"A loner who gets lonely," she said. "Bet you've got a woman in every port."

"Not exactly," I said. "I've had my share, but right now I'm unattached."

"Me too," she said.

I could have sworn I saw a sparkle in her eye when she said that. She didn't wink. Maybe it was a reflection.

"My job makes it hard to sustain a relationship," she said.

"My lifestyle makes it hard to sustain a relationship," I told her.

"Your lifestyle or all the trouble you keep finding yourself in?" she asked.

"That too," I said. "It never starts out that way, but I'm a trouble magnet."

"Don't kid yourself," she said. "Some of it is self-inflicted."

"Sure, some of it," I said.

"You had some trouble with the IRS years ago," she said. "Spent a few days in a city lockup."

"I made complete restitution and then some," I told her.

"Cops had you nailed down here on a dope possession charge," she said. "Somehow you got off easy."

"I had a good lawyer," I said. "Last I knew she was in a nut hut."

"Is that how all your ex-lovers end up? Broken and crazy?"

"Of course not," I said. "And you know way too much about me. You're creeping me out."

"I apologize," she said. "I guess I was just bragging about how much I've learned, even without much of an electronic footprint."

"Good work, agent Brody," I said. "Do you have a first name?"

"Meredith," she said. "But please don't call me that. Nobody does."

"I thought using your last name was a guy thing," I said. "Call me Breeze."

"The FBI is very male dominated," she said. "I've been Brody since I joined."

"Is that why you wear your hair so short? To be like one of the guys?"

"It's just easier this way," she said. "Trust me. I'm all girl."

Our conversation was almost flirtatious. It was too personal for two people who'd just met. She'd made me her life's mission. Now she wanted to impress me with how much she knew about me. At the same time, she was letting me know that her interest might be something more. I'd been caught off guard again. She'd drawn me into a personal conversation without me even knowing it. She was probably a profiler as well. She had the upper hand. I didn't know what to say next.

ED ROBINSON

"It's been a pleasure to meet you, Breeze," she said. "Good to know you're not a real ghost."

"So now what?" I asked. "You're just going to follow me around until Bobby gets better or dies?"

"I can't watch you forever," she admitted. "But now that I've found you, I thought maybe we could get to know each other. It would help to pass the time."

"I doubt your employer would approve," I said. "Besides, I'm the bad guy, right?"

"You don't seem as dangerous as people think," she said. "What happened down there in Guatemala?"

"Long story," I said. "Nothing that I'm proud of."

"He has a conscience too," she said.

"Look, the FBI is wasting their time," I said. "I'm a nobody. I'd like to stay that way."

"Right now it's my time," she said. "I deem you to be a somebody."

"Suit yourself," I said. "As soon as I can get re-provisioned, I'm out of here. Try to keep up."

"You're on," she replied.

"Good night, Breeze."

"Later, Brody."

I waved to Jennifer on the way out. Her look said I'm sorry. I just kept walking. I went back to my boat and took stock of my supplies. I needed to pick up some things. I wondered if Brody would follow me to the store. I'd picked up a shadow. She was no Holly in the looks department, but she was attractive enough. At first, she'd come across as stern and serious, but her smile and the twinkle in her eye told a different story. What the hell, I thought. She probably looks nice in a bikini. If she followed me back to Pelican Bay, I couldn't stop her.

On the other hand, if I left when she wasn't watching, I could lose her by going somewhere else. Maybe her feminine attentions were a ruse. She might be trying to win me over, make it easier for her to keep tabs on me. The more I thought about it, the more I was convinced. They probably taught that stuff in G-man school. She was playing me.

I sat down with my charts and started looking for a good place to ditch my tail. I knew she would never find me in the Everglades, but I just couldn't bring myself to go back there. I could possibly avoid her in Goodland, but my friend Shirley had died there. I didn't want the bad memories. I looked north. Chadwick Cove was too open to prying eyes. The Manatee River was a possibility. Anything north of there was new territory for me. I could run up the Anclote River to Tarpon Springs. I could hide in Crystal River.

I thought about how I'd do it. If I hung around where I was, sooner or later she'd go to shore. I'd be watching. I'd wait until she was on land, maybe taking a shower or whatever, then I'd bolt. She couldn't be sure which way I went. She'd most likely go to Pelican Bay looking for me. If I wasn't there, she'd only be guessing where I might have gone. I'd have a good head start. I noticed a dinghy coming into the mooring field. The short dark hair told me it was Brody. She tied up to an older Mainship 34 and climbed aboard. She waved in my direction. I waved back.

Her boat was a slow trawler like mine. Mainship had built a variety of them in the late seventies and early eighties. They still made the larger ones. Her speed would depend on engine size. If I couldn't outrun her, I'd have to outsmart her. For some reason, I couldn't make up my mind how to do that. I considered running up to Tarpon Springs and jumping across the Gulf to the Panhandle. She'd never expect that, and wouldn't be likely to follow. I kept mulling it over.

I went to bed thinking about Brody. The more I pictured her in my mind, the prettier she became. At the bar, she'd worn tight fitting shorts that came down to the knee. Her white shirt was crisp and buttoned up high. I pictured her on the beach wearing much less. I pictured her with longer hair. I remembered Joy. She'd had really short blond hair. Her face wasn't the prettiest, but we'd had a lot of fun together. Joy had a nice ass. So did Brody. Maybe I was being premature about her. Maybe she really was interested in me. She'd certainly invested a lot of time and effort finding me.

I tried to listen to my gut, but my sixth sense was stuck in neutral. Brody had popped into my life out of nowhere. I didn't have enough to go on, yet. I couldn't determine her true intentions. The only way to get to the bottom of things was to spend more time with her. I could always ditch her later. If I figured out that she was just a cop doing her job, I'd be in the wind before she knew what happened. With the matter settled, at least temporarily, I drifted off to sleep.

I was awakened in the morning by a knock on my hull. Brody was there in her dinghy.

"Care to take a girl to breakfast?" she asked.

"Hold on a minute," I yelled.

I dressed hastily and went out to greet her. She looked bright-eyed and ready to face the day.

"I need to at least brush my teeth," I said.

"Mind if I come aboard?"

"Make yourself at home," I said. "I'll just be a minute."

She poked around while I got ready.

"I wanted something more like this," she said. "But I couldn't find a good one in my price range."

"That's a decent boat you have," I said. "Not fancy, but serviceable. Are you going to keep it after this is over?"

"I haven't decided yet," she said. "It's okay for one, but a bit small for two."

"How much boating experience do you have?"

"Some," she said. "Smaller outboard boats."

"A single screw trawler is a different animal than an outboard," I told her.

"Wherever you're planning on going, you could take me with you," she suggested. "You could teach me. Be a whole lot easier than me following you in my boat."

"Uh, no," I said. "I haven't decided what your motives are yet. Just met you yesterday."

"That's okay," she said. "I haven't decided what my motives are either."

"Still wondering if I'm a monstrous felon?"

"Maybe, but I'm holding out for a rugged individual who's been dealt some bad cards," she said. "You're certainly nothing like any man I've ever met."

"All part of my charm, Brody," I said with a wink. "Let's go eat."

I took her to Bonita Bills. She didn't turn her nose up at the greasy spoon aspect of the place. You order breakfast at the bar, and they bring it out to you. As many patrons were drinking beer as those that were drinking coffee.

"So what's your plan?" she asked.

"Get some groceries," I said. "Head on out."

"Where to?"

"I guess you'll have to figure that out for yourself," I said.

"Oh come on, Breeze," she said. "You trying to lose me already?"

"It will be a test for you," I said. "An easy one. I don't even know if you can drive that boat."

"How do we get groceries around here?"

"You've got two choices by dinghy," I began. "Topps is close, but I'd avoid it. It's not safe for a single woman."

"Come with me then," she said.

"I've got my own reasons to avoid it," I said.

"What's our other option?"

"Up the river to Snook Bight Marina," I said. "There's a Publix right behind it."

"How far up the river?"

"A couple miles," I said. "It's a long dinghy ride."

"I'll need some more gas," she said.

"Moss Marine, on the other side of the bridge," I told her. "You can get diesel there too if you need it."

"Depends on how far we're going," she said, smiling.

Her eyes did that twinkle thing again. It happened whenever she smiled.

"How do you do that?" I asked.

"Do what?"

"Whenever you smile, your eyes sparkle," I said.

"You're the first person to tell me that," she said.

"I tend to look people in the eye," I said. "They say the eyes are the window to the soul."

"Is that why you always wear sunglasses?" she asked. "To hide your soul?"

"We're in the sunshine state," I said, taking off my shades.

She looked directly into my eyes, studying them. She held her stare for a long time.

"Your eyes are as blue as the waters of the Bahamas," she said. "You've got the ocean in your soul."

"I'd say that's a fair assessment," I said. "The water is my life. That and my old boat."

"It all sounds so romantic," she said.

"It's not all dolphins and sunsets. It comes with its own hardships."

"Would you trade it?" she asked.

"Not for anything in the world."

"I thought I had you figured out," she said. "But I was wrong."

"How's that?"

"I knew you'd be salty and a little bit rough," she said. "But underneath hides a sensitive man. Rare combination these days."

"I yam what I yam," I said, using my best Popeye impersonation.

"And a sense of humor too," she said. "How come some salty sailor girl hasn't swept you up?"

I thought of Holly. She was the saltiest sailor girl I'd ever met, but she was none of Brody's business. I decided to keep my history with women to myself. Brody knew too much about me already. Wherever this budding relationship went, it could do without the baggage of my ex-lovers. I wouldn't ask about hers either.

"I guess I haven't met the right one yet," I said. "There's always hope."

"You're not getting any younger," she said.

"No shit," I said. "They teach you that in FBI school?"

"I didn't mean any harm," she said. "I still find you incredibly attractive, in a roguish sort of way."

"This is where I'm supposed to admit I'm attracted to you, right?"

"Well? You are, aren't you?"

"Okay, I confess," I said. "I didn't like the short hair at first. You came across as some stiff-necked authoritarian. I've changed my opinion since my first impression."

"To what?"

"Your smile and that eye twinkling thing are endearing," I said. "I bet you look nice in a bikini. You're growing on me."

"I only brought a one-piece," she said.

"That will never do," I said. "You'll need to visit one of the surf shops before we leave. It's a strict rule I have."

"The rogue has rules," she said. "What are Breeze's ten commandments?"

"Not that many," I said. "There's the bikini thing. I try not to start drinking until five. I never miss the sunset if I can help it. The care of my boat is always priority number one. That's about it."

"No Golden Rule?"

"Sometimes I have to do unto others," I said. "Folks get what they deserve, good or bad."

"Sounds ominous."

"It's been the source of most of my troubles," I said. "It's time to re-assess that. Like you said, I'm not getting any younger."

"What is it you want out of life?" she asked.

Her concern seemed genuine. Her line of inquiry wasn't that of an FBI agent. I looked into her eyes again. Was she a friend or a foe?

"I want to be left alone, but not be alone," I said. "If that makes any sense."

"You want a woman who's willing to live like you do," she said. "Is that it?"

"That's been the dream," I admitted. "Preferably anchored near some idyllic island in the Caribbean. Hasn't worked out so far."

"That's quite the romantic vision you have," she said.

"There's more to it than that," I said. "It can be tough, especially on a woman."

"You're showing your chauvinism," she said. "How tough can it be to lay on the beach naked and eat fish for dinner?"

"It's not that easy," I told her. "Call it sensitive chauvinism if you like. Most women can't take it for long."

"I bet I could," she said.

We looked at each other. She smiled and sparkled.

"You're a piece of work, Brody," I said. "We met like five minutes ago and already you're insinuating your way into my life."

"Is that a bad thing?"

"I haven't decided yet," I answered truthfully. "Maybe you're softening me up so I'll be easier to extradite to Guatemala."

"Maybe you're charming me so it will be harder for me to take you in," she said.

"I might have thought of that if I was a little smarter," I said. "Is it working?"

"You are both smart and charming," she said. "But there's something else about you. I can't put my finger on it. It's bewildering. Bewitching even."

I almost used the term *animal magnetism*. I stopped short. A quick memory of me thrashing Bobby flashed through my mind. Brody knew what happened. She knew Bobby was in bad shape, thanks to me. She was already hunting me when it happened, even though I wasn't wanted for any crimes at the time. She knew that I was a potentially dangerous man, yet she was blatantly flirting with me. Maybe she hadn't taken a sabbatical from her job just to prove to herself that she could find me. Maybe I was her obsession. That could prove dangerous to me, yet there I sat, flirting back. I changed the subject.

"Let's go get some groceries," I said. "Then we can hit the bikini store."

Sixteen

We took separate dinghies to Publix so we'd have room for all of our groceries. After we each put our stuff away, we rode together to the dinghy dock. The surf shops were only a few blocks away. She picked out some sexy little numbers and tried them on. I was hoping to see them on her, but she came out of the dressing room fully clothed. She said they fit just fine. The body reveal would have to wait.

I tried to guess her age. Her body was firm and made me think late thirties at first. After a closer look, the fine lines made me think mid-forties. Not that she was old looking, she was simply more mature than I'd first thought. When she flashed that smile, she could pass for twenty-nine. I started putting some effort into making her smile, cracking jokes whenever I could think of one. She told some jokes of her own, matching my wit easily. Considering our situation, it was a surprisingly carefree day.

We dawdled in town so long, the hour grew too late to leave the harbor. We walked up Old San Carlos Boulevard to Zushi Zushi. We ordered sushi and a beer. Any onlooker would have thought we were lovers. We'd only known each other for twenty-four hours. Somehow, we'd found comfort in each other's company. I forgot that she was a law enforcement officer, at least for a little while.

I remembered as I dropped her at her boat. She asked if I wanted to come aboard. I wanted to step back so I could think things through. I was enjoying being with her, but it was happening too fast. I needed to be wary, in case some type of trap was being set. I begged off and said good night. I tried to make sense of what was going on.

The idea that the woman who had tracked me down had then found me too irresistible to arrest was absurd. What kind of game were we playing then? Was she hoping to get her rocks off before putting the cuffs on me? What if Bobby held on for months, or even years? She couldn't play her game forever. On the other hand, sitting with her, looking into her eyes, made me feel good. It was nice. She was nice. If the call came and her orders were to arrest me, would she go through with it?

I was playing with fire, and I knew it. I thought I should run. I thought I should pull up anchor and go somewhere far away. I should have gone somewhere that she'd never consider, but that's not what I did. I went to Pelican Bay. I left at four in the morning. She'd wake up and I'd be gone. She'd have no choice but to check Pelican Bay first if she could make it that far. Then she'd be on my turf. She'd realize that I could escape at any time, but that I'd made it easy for her to find me. Her reaction would give me a better sense of her motives. If she failed the test then she wasn't worthy.

I settled into my usual anchoring spot and waited. She was only a few hours behind me. I watched her pick her way into the unfamiliar channel. She made it through, then hesitated. She hovered just off the end of the sandbar at the end of the channel. I saw her go forward and release her anchor. When her boat settled on the chain, it floated barely inside the entrance. To other boaters, it was an asshole thing to do. I realized what she was up to. It was my only way out. To leave the bay I'd have to go right past her. I'd be impossible to miss. It was an excellent strategy on her part. I had tried to sneak out the back way once and ran aground. It could be done on an extremely high tide, but I didn't care to risk it.

She came right over in her dinghy. She was wearing a pink bikini top. She had cut-off shorts on over the bottoms. They weren't buttoned and the zipper was open. It was sexy as hell. She wore a floppy hat to keep the sun off her face.

"Ready to go to the beach?" she asked.

"You passed the test," I said. "I give you an A-plus."

"Put some swim shorts on," she said. "Let's go."

"Pretty clever how you anchored," I said.

"I thought so," she said.

"The tour boats will yell at you for blocking the channel."

"Not if I'm on the beach," she said. "We going or not?"

She gave me no lecture on leaving in the wee hours of the morning. There was no condemnation for trying to ditch her, even though I'd made myself easy to find. She acted like nothing ever happened, like we planned it this way. We took her dinghy. She let me drive. We cut through Murdock Bayou and followed the mangrove shoreline to a tunnel entrance.

"They call this the Tunnel of Love," I told her.

"It's beautiful," she said.

"Wait until you see the other side."

We ducked under low branches and wove our way through the tunnel. It emptied us into a lake. We beached the dinghy and stepped across some seagrass to the Gulf side beach. The view took her breath away. She walked onto the sand and pulled her shorts off. That view took my breath away. She had those little dimples on either side of her lower back. Her ass was even nicer than I'd imagined. She turned to look at me staring at her. Her medium sized breasts were high and firm.

"It's amazing," she said.

"You look really great in that bikini," I said.

"Take your shirt off," she said. "Come join me."

I did as she suggested. We ran out into the Gulf together and dove in. We stood up on a sandbar. I found a sand dollar and handed it to her.

"This is how you live?" she asked. "You can do this every day?"

"When the weather is nice," I said. "I come over here and take a little jog on the beach. Swim for a bit. Catch some rays."

"Where are the people?"

"This is my own private beach most of the time," I said. "Some cruisers come here sometimes."

"It's hard to believe there's still a place like this in Florida," she said.

"Next best thing to the Bahamas," I said.

"It feels like we're the only two people on earth," she said. "Thank you."

"Don't thank me," I said. "You found your way here all by yourself."

"You could have run," she said. "But you didn't. Not really."

"I almost did," I said. "I thought real hard about it."

"Why didn't you?" she said. "What stopped you?"

"You have a way of getting right to the heart of the matter," I said. "No beating around the bush."

"There's no one here but us," she said. "You can tell me."

"I always run," I said. "It's my first instinct. From trouble, from relationships, from my own fears. It's gotten easy to just run away."

"What's different this time?"

"Something about you, Brody," I said. "I need to know if you're worth facing my fears."

"You can run at any time," she said. "I won't stop you, if that makes you feel any better."

"After everything you went through to find me?" I asked. "You'd just let me motor out of here?"

"That's not what I want," she said. "But the choice is yours."

"What will your bosses say?"

"Let me worry about that," she said.

"I want to stay here for a while," I said. "You're welcome to stay too. I'd like for you to stay."

She came to me in the waist deep water. She took both my hands and looked into my eyes. She kissed me softly. We held the kiss for a long time. I enjoyed it very much. I saw her differently after that kiss. Suddenly, she was a beauty. Her smile, her eyes, her figure, they came together to draw me in. I still knew that I was playing with fire. Now we'd thrown gasoline on it. The fire was dangerous, but mesmerizing.

We lay on the beach and watched the clouds. Tiny waves lapped at the shore. We didn't speak for an hour or more. We just soaked up the sun. At that moment, the rest of the world didn't matter. We had our own little world of sun, sand, and saltwater. I hadn't been so happy to just be, in a long time. Something about sharing my world with a woman made it better.

"This is nice," she said. "I could stay here forever."

"Me too, except I'm getting hungry," I said. "Let's go fix some dinner."

The tide had receded. On the way back through the tunnel, we had to get out of the dinghy and pull it through the shallow spots. Brody didn't seem to mind the muck under her feet. We both got sweaty and dirty. Back on the boat, I suggested a deck shower. She looked around. Her boat was the only other one in the bay. The pink bikini hit the deck. She hosed herself off then held the hose out to me. She looked down at my swim trunks. Normally I would have been concerned about shrinkage, but Breeze Junior had stirred while I watched Brody shower. The swim trunks hit the deck.

She gave me a few minutes to hose off the salt before taking me by the hand. She pulled me inside. I kicked the table away from the settee and took her right there in the salon. It felt taboo, which made it exciting. The law lady was screwing the target of her investigation. I'd been looking at her body all day. Now I got to feel her and taste her. I was not disappointed. It felt right.

She had no clothes with her except the bikini. I gave her a shirt and a pair of boxers to put on. We each grabbed a beer and sat on the back deck.

"I'm starving," I said.

"I'll cook," she said. "What do you have?"

"See for yourself," I said.

She opened the freezer.

"Beef, beef, and more beef," she said.

"There should be some fish in there if you'd rather have that," I said.

"It will take some time to thaw," she said. "Do you have any cheese and crackers in the meantime?"

"Port wine cheese in the fridge," I said. "Crackers in the pantry."

She brought the fish outside to thaw. We sat and nibbled crackers and drank our beers. It had been a satisfying day. It was the kind of day I had imagined in my dreams.

"Quite the life you have here, Breeze," she said. "I'm telling you, I could live like this."

"You'll be doing it by yourself if I'm in a Guatemalan jail," I said. "Or with someone else."

"Let's not ruin a perfect day," she said. "Let's stay in this moment."

We changed the subject. I told her about some of the places I'd been aboard *Leap of Faith*. I couldn't even remember all of them. I'd put a lot of miles under her keel over the years. I took her on a mental tour of the Bahamas, from the Berry Islands down through the Exumas. I told her about Luperon, leaving out any mention of the ex-lover who lived there. I didn't mention Holly when I told her about the beautiful islands I'd visited. I told her about being detained in Cuba. I didn't tell her about the pretty girl I'd smuggled back into the states. I told her about the Virgin Islands, not mentioning that I'd spread my wife's ashes there. I didn't want Brody and Breeze to be haunted by the ghosts of my past. I wanted a clean slate.

Her phone rang. She didn't say much. I couldn't hear the voice of the caller. She hung up.

"That was the embassy," she said.

"And?"

"Mr. Beard's family has asked that he not be resuscitated when the time comes. It won't be much longer."

"Not good news," I said. "What are you going to do?"

"This," she said.

She again took my hand and led me inside, this time to my bunk. She took the lead and I let her. There was an urgency to her lovemaking, like she was afraid it would be our last time. When she was finished, she held me close for a long time. I felt close to her. It was natural. We'd met a few days prior, but I was totally at ease with her. I couldn't bring myself to worry about the consequences. I was enjoying her so much.

We watched the last few seconds of the sunset. She gave me a quick kiss as it blinked out. She smiled and her eyes sparkled. Then she cooked the fish. We forgot about the fate of Bobby Beard.

Seventeen

The next day we re-anchored her boat in a more appropriate spot. We brought it closer to mine. She moved some of her clothes and lady stuff onto *Leap of Faith*. It should have felt weird, but it didn't. I lowered my guard somewhat. There was no need to worry about the FBI showing up. The FBI was living on my boat. Between the two of us, we had enough food to last for a month or more. She had plenty of fresh water too.

We spent our days fishing, swimming and soaking up the sun. We spent our nights drinking and making love. She was an imaginative cook. She used whatever she could find in our cupboards to throw together something different every night. We eventually ran out of fresh fruit and vegetables. The last of the bread was moldy. We had no milk. She didn't complain. The only thing she insisted on were more frequent showers. When I was alone, I wouldn't take a real shower for a week or more. When I was alone, I didn't have to worry about smelling nice for a pretty lady that wanted to make love every night. We had the extra water from her boat though, so regular showers we took.

We knew the time would come, but we were both disappointed when the water supply was gone. We'd been living in our own world. We'd been sharing a life that few would ever know. We'd been caring for each other without distraction. Now we had to go back to civilization. We didn't want to go.

"I just want to tell you, Breeze," she said. "I'm so grateful to you for this time. I've never been so happy. You've changed me."

"You weren't always this awesome?" I asked.

"Well, no," she admitted. "It's a dog-eat-dog world out there. My job magnifies that a million times. It's all male ego, politics, and bullshit. The stress eats at you, but the weight of it all has disappeared. Thanks to you."

"You'll have to go back sooner or later," I said.

"I don't want to think about that," she said. "Not yet."

"You've changed me too," I said.

"You weren't always this awesome either?" she asked.

"It's not that," I said. "But I'm nervous about telling you."

"I know it's been quick," she said. "But we've gotten so close. No need to be nervous now."

"There're a lot of things you don't know about me," I said. "But know this. You have my heart and soul. I don't know how it happened, but I've never been able to give of myself like I want to do for you. That's a monumental change. You must be something special."

"I don't care about your past," she said. "I only care about us right here and right now."

"That's a beautiful sentiment that I totally agree with," I said. "But what happens when our bubble bursts?"

"It'll work out," she said. "Have faith."

"Leap of Faith," I said. "Takes on a new meaning with you."

She smiled and sparkled. I knew that I loved her. I also knew that we'd have to face reality when Bobby died. I didn't know if we could survive it.

We took both boats back to Fort Myers Beach. We decided we'd put hers in a marina and list it with a broker. It wouldn't bring much, but we didn't need two boats anymore. She had few personal belongings on board, which was surprising. She wasn't like most women in that regard. We worked together to find places to store all of her stuff aboard my boat. Other than her shampoo and conditioner, she did nothing to make my boat more feminine. Her hair had grown out a little over the past month. It still was too short, but she hadn't made a move to cut it, so that was promising.

We went about the business of loading water, fuel and groceries. We ate out several nights in a row, but avoided the Upper Deck. My fling with Jennifer was past history. I deservedly felt guilty for coming between her and Bobby. It may have worked out well for Jennifer, but it led to disaster for Bobby and me. It had also contributed to Brody finding me. That was both good and bad.

After three days we were both itching to leave. The noise and annoyance of Fort Myers Beach was getting to us. We even failed to make love a couple of nights while we were there. That couldn't stand. We couldn't wait to get back to the peace and love of our private paradise. We took one last hot shower on shore before dropping the mooring ball and heading out of the harbor.

We broke our sex drought a few minutes after anchoring. We had a few neighbors this time. Two sailboats and one trawler had arrived while we were gone. As was my habit, I kept close surveillance on them until I was satisfied that they were no threat. I asked Brody to assist me. She had observation skills from her training, but little knowledge of life on the water. I trained her in the ways of Breeze. We made a game of building an entire life story for each captain and crew that arrived.

We quickly fell back into the rhythm of the island. We never tired of the beach, the dolphins or the manatees. We started getting regular afternoon thunderstorms that are common in Florida. We anticipated them. As soon as it started raining, we ran out on deck to rinse off in the cool fresh water. If our neighbors were too close, we wore bathing suits. If not, we were naked. I rigged up a rain catching system to top off our water tanks. We could then stay away from the real world for much longer.

Other than the specter of Bobby's imminent death hanging over us, life was as perfect as it could be. We didn't talk about it. I tried not to think about it. I did a good job of ignoring it until the dream returned. It was the three doors again. I knew who was behind the first two doors. I had to open the third this time. I couldn't help myself. I was compelled to see who was behind it. My fears were confirmed. I opened the door. It was Bobby. Just like the other two, he was a million miles away. I could see him, but I couldn't reach him. He was gone.

I sat straight up in bed, waking with a terrible foreboding feeling. What would it mean for me and Brody? She woke up too.

"What's wrong?" she asked.

"Just a bad dream," I said.

I started to get out of bed but she grabbed me.

"Stay with me," she said. "Let me hold you."

We embraced under the covers. We were in a warm, safe place. The longer we stayed alone together, the more I dreaded going back. The embrace turned to something more. We made soft, sweet love. We were detached from everything, except each other. Our boat had become another planet, where we avoided all of the distractions of modern life. The dream had intruded on our safety. Bobby's death lurked like a silent killer, waiting to strike down our newfound partnership.

Brody got a phone call early the next morning. When she hung up, I knew.

"Bobby's dead," I said.

"How did you know?"

"I saw it in the dream last night," I told her.

"I know it's bad," she said. "But you're connected to the universe somehow. You saw the future."

"Not really," I said. "I saw it as soon as he passed. I could feel it. I knew."

"It's still some kind of extra-sensory perception," she said.

"But what will it mean for us?"

That was the big question. What would Brody do? What would the FBI do? I assumed they knew exactly where I was. I wanted her to reassure me somehow. I wanted to run, but leaving her would be awfully hard to do. We'd come too far together. I knew when we first met that this day would come. I knew that I should have disappeared right from the start, but I couldn't do it. I'd taken a leap of faith with Brody. I couldn't turn my back on her. Would she turn her back on me?

"Sit down, Breeze," she said. "Relax. Let's talk this through."

"Are you going to arrest me?"

"It doesn't work like that," she said. "The FBI can make arrests if they witness a crime being committed, or if they are reasonably sure the person being arrested has broken a U. S. law. Your case would be the responsibility of Guatemalan law enforcement."

"What if they want to have me extradited?"

"They'll make a request through the Justice Department," she said.

"Then what?"

"It would eventually work its way back to my office," she said. "But any local law agency could bring you in."

"How long do I have?"

"It depends on how fast they move down in Guatemala," she said. "If an extradition order comes down, I'll find out about it."

"I won't go voluntarily," I told her. "Not even for questioning. I won't speak to the FBI. I won't be returned to Guatemala. I'll never face trial down there."

"The alternative is to run and hide," she said. "Your first instinct."

"I'm not technically wanted yet," I said. "My passport is still good. I may have time to get out of the country. Would they pursue me then? How hard would they look for me?"

"The FBI doesn't have the resources to hunt the four corners of the globe looking for someone like you," she said. "It won't be that high of a priority. No offense intended."

"None taken," I said. "So as long as I stay out of trouble, I won't be found, right?"

"Your track record suggests that could be difficult," she said.

"Not with your help," I said. "You could keep me on the straight and narrow."

"I have my passport," she said.

"Will you come with me?"

It felt like a marriage proposal. I was asking her to leave her entire life behind. I was asking her to aid and abet a known criminal. If she said no, I'd still run, but I'd be a broken man. I tried to make the connection between my horrible episode with Bobby, and finding a way to unlock my heart. Since my wife's death, I'd stayed locked inside myself. Even when I was with another woman, I had never been able to fully let go. I'd never truly given of myself. Brody was changing that. If she said no, my chance to regain my humanity would go with her. I desperately wanted to hold onto the love we'd discovered, that I'd discovered within myself.

She came to me and put her head on my chest. She didn't speak for a minute. Finally, she lifted her head and looked into my eyes. She didn't smile. She didn't sparkle.

"I could hear your heart beating," she said. "I never want to lose that."

"You'll come with me?"

"I'm terrified, Breeze," she said. "I can't do this, but I want it so bad. I want you so bad."

"It'll work out," I told her. "Leap of faith and all that."

"It's crazy," she said. "I'm an FBI agent. I can't go on the run."

"I'm real good at it," I assured her. "We'll find that perfect island. Lay naked on the beach and eat fish every night."

She went out on the back deck and looked out over the water. She stood there with her hands on her hips and stared. I stood beside her and put my arm around her shoulders. An eagle soared overhead. It circled us a few times before departing.

"It's good luck to see an eagle," I told her. "It's a sign."

"Freedom," she said. "The eagle represents freedom."

"I think you're starting to understand," I said.

"Will you love me, Breeze," she asked. "I mean really love me?"

"I already do," I said. "You know that."

"Say it."

"I love you, Brody," I said.

"I love you, Breeze."

She had tears running down her cheeks. I wasn't sure what that meant. Was she happy or sad? Maybe she was just afraid. Loving me contradicted everything she stood for. Running off with me was the unknown. It was no small leap. It was jumping out of a plane with no parachute. Part of me wanted to give her a way out, but I couldn't do it.

"Brody?"

"God damn you, Breeze," she said. "I'll go with you."

"You've made me a very happy man," I said.

"I must be out of my mind," she said. "Running from the freaking FBI."

"They couldn't find me before," I said.

"I found you," she said.

"Yeah," I said. "But now you're on my side."

"I am," she said. "Take me away to paradise."

Eighteen

Back in Fort Myers Beach, we accepted a lowball offer on Brody's boat. I instructed her to spend only cash and to never use a credit or debit card. She knew the drill. She told me that her phone was spook proof. It couldn't be tracked using traditional methods. It was something that the CIA had developed. Whenever she made a call, it would bounce off of hundreds of towers. Whoever was pinging it would think she was far from her actual location. I didn't trust the technology, but she assured me it was safe. We took no other electronic devices with us.

We loaded up with groceries. We filled the water tanks. We took hot showers. I stopped for fuel on the way out of the harbor. We left it all behind. We left Fort Myers Beach, Pelican Bay, and the FBI in our rearview mirror. Brody's old life was over. Our life together was about to really begin. She had made a commitment stronger than any wedding vows. I couldn't be happier about it, but she was justifiably nervous. Staying on the run was old hat for me. She had always been on the other side of the law. We used that to our advantage.

She had friends at her old workplace. If something relevant came across their desks, they'd contact her. We'd be able to stay a step ahead of them. We'd know if and when they wanted to find us. We checked into the Bahamas in Bimini. If the State Department flagged my passport, they'd know where we were. They wouldn't know where we'd go after that. The possibilities were endless.

We chose Hoffman's Cay in the Berry Islands. It was remote, but within cell range of Great Harbor's tower. We used the shallow draft route to reach the anchorage on the west side of the island. It was out of reach for deeper draft boats. *Miss Leap* could barely make it in on high tide. We were all alone. There had been no call from anyone at the FBI.

We had a pretty white sand beach. We had a blue hole. We had a dozen other islands to explore. Best of all, we had each other. We ate, we drank, and made love in the tropical sun. We had a million stars over us each night. We discussed additional exotic locations that we'd like to visit. A month went in the blink of an eye. There were no phone calls.

We made a run down to Chub Cay to take on water. The cell signal was strong. Brody checked her messages. There were none from the FBI. It was a curious thing. Bobby had been dead for more than a month. As far as we could tell, there had been no request for extradition. I might be persona non grata in Guatemala, but no one else was looking for me. We relaxed even more.

Brody had developed a deep tan. Her hair was now almost down to her shoulders. I loved the way she looked. I took her to Nassau to go shopping. She picked out some cute sundresses and a few more bikinis. We ate an expensive meal at a fancy restaurant. We paid for everything in cash.

We stopped at Big Majors to see the swimming pigs. We ate dinner at the Staniel Cay Yacht Club. We got a mooring ball at Warderick Wells in the Exumas Land and Sea

Park. Cell coverage was almost non-existent, but we had stopped caring so much. The anticipated call hadn't come. We went on with our life. We stayed on that ball for weeks. We backtracked to Staniel to take on water and pick up some groceries. Over dinner, the subject of my status came up.

"Aren't you curious?" she asked me.

"No news is good news," I said.

"It's been bugging me," she said. "I'd really like to know what's going on."

"Either I'm not a wanted man," I said. "Or your friends at the FBI aren't talking to you. Maybe they've figured out that you switched teams."

"We used our passports in Bimini," she said.

"Doesn't mean they know where we are now," I said.

"If we leave the Bahamas we'll have to use our passports again," she said. "I told you that everyone leaves a trace, no matter how hard you try to hide."

"So we stay in the Bahamas," I offered. "Or we could go back to Florida and not check in. They'll think we're still in the Bahamas."

"We don't even know if they're looking for us," she said.

"Been there, done that," I told her. "The prudent thing to do is stay a ghost, whether they're after you or not."

"We can't live like that forever," she said.

"I beg to differ," I said. "We've got enough money. The boat is running great, and we have each other. We can stay gone indefinitely."

"Don't get me wrong," she said. "I'm loving every minute of this. I'm just curious."

"You're the G-man," I said. "There's got to be a way to find out."

"It can wait until tomorrow," she said. "I want to screw your brains out tonight. One more day before I make contact with the real world."

"This is our world," I told her. "It's as real as we want it to be. We don't need anything else."

"You're the sweetest man," she said. "Wasn't in your profile."

"I can name a bunch of people who would disagree with that assessment."

"Right here and right now," she said. "That's all that matters."

We stifled her curiosity with sex. Whenever we were together like that, nothing else existed. There was no Bobby Beard, no FBI, no extradition orders, no past and no future. We lived in that moment. It was a powerful drug. I knew that our pace would slow, but I soaked up every minute of it.

In the morning, she made the call. Her co-worker said that there was no extradition order. They hadn't heard from anyone at the State Department or the Guatemalan government. The death of Bobby Beard wasn't on their radar at all. Brody was relieved. I was too, but now my curiosity was peaked. Why not? You don't just murder an American citizen in a foreign country without someone caring. Wouldn't his family want justice?

My guilt for what I had done was renewed. I had put it all out of my mind for the past three months. I'd been consumed with Brody. She had become my entire world. I felt bad for Bobby and his family, but I couldn't go back and fix it. What I did have was a reason to move on. I had a new life with Brody. I knew it was real. She'd given up everything she'd ever known to be with me. She'd chosen me over everything else, despite what I'd done.

"Call some people down there in Guatemala," I said. "Try the hospital and the embassy. Somebody has to know what the deal is."

"Not yet," she said. "Let's enjoy this. No one is looking for you. Let's move on from it."

So we moved on. We began a quest to locate that perfect island. We stopped at every Cay that had a decent anchorage. Each one was more beautiful than the last. Brody grew more beautiful in my eyes with each passing day. Her hair was getting longer. Her tan got darker and darker. I relished the lighter spots that her bikinis covered. My natural inhibitions fell away. We were Adam and Eve in the Garden of Eden. We were happy, and those days quickly passed by. We spent some time in George Town to take on more supplies. We got fuel and water. We continued south to Long Island. We explored the Jumentos Cays and the Ragged Islands. These were mostly undeveloped. The water surrounding them was stunning. We rarely saw another boat.

The only fly in the ointment was my desire to know why no one was looking for me. Was law enforcement in Guatemala so poor that they didn't care what happened? Had Brody's coworker misled her? That was a possibility we hadn't considered. Maybe they were looking for me. Making us think that we were free would be a clever ploy. It stuck in the back of my mind for weeks. Eventually, it worked its way to the front. I wanted to know.

We were anchored in Sapodilla Bay in the Turks and Caicos. I talked it over with Brody.

"Pretend you're still an agent," I said. "Call everybody and anybody who might know something."

"You won't let it go, will you?"

"It's not paranoia if someone is really out to get you," I said.

"I'll see what I can do," she said.

She spent hours calling all over the place. She confirmed with a contact in the State Department that no extradition order existed. She talked to the American embassy in Guatemala. She called the hospital and various Guatemalan law enforcement agencies. She even called Texan Bay Marina. The story was starting to come together. When she finished with the last call, she had me sit down on the settee. She had a satisfied look on her face. She was good at interrogation. She'd gotten the information she needed.

"They don't know who you are," she said.

"How is that possible?"

"No one at the marina gave you up," she said.

"Impossible," I said.

"Nope," she said. "Big Mike didn't tell anyone who you were. No one else that was questioned mentioned your name. They all played dumb. I understand that some of the witnesses had already left the area. Important witnesses."

"I don't know what to say," I said. "I caused those people a lot of grief."

"There's more," she said. "Bobby spoke."

"What did he say?"

"His family was there," she said. "They were screaming for justice. He was taken off the machines. That's when he spoke."

"Come on, Brody," I said. "Tell me what he said."

"It was my fault," she said. "He told his family that it was his fault. There was no reason to look any further for his assailant."

I tried to sort out my conflicting feelings. Bobby had exonerated me of my guilt. That poor, dumb son-of-a-bitch had taken the blame. I was a free man. I juggled my happiness with my sadness for Bobby. I was grateful for those four words. *It was my fault.*

"You can now move about the planet freely," said Brody.

She smiled and sparkled.

"As long as you go with me," I said.

"Any place you care to go."

We were free to pursue our shared dream. It had once been my dream alone. It was finally coming true. We'd keep looking for our perfect island. We'd live in love and happiness, far removed from the rest of the world.

It was all I ever wanted.

Author's Thoughts

I envision Breeze and Brody becoming as adventurous a team as Breeze and Holly were. The series isn't over yet. You know that Breeze can't stay out of trouble for long.

As usual, any names of public or private persons are used fictitiously.

Feel free to send feedback, ideas or suggestions to kimandedrobinson@gmail.com

Special thanks to **Bobby Beard** for allowing me to take great liberties with his character. I hope he got his money's worth.

More thanks to **Jennifer Mossburg** for allowing me to create a character based on her. I hope I did her justice. She's good people.

If you'd like to have your name in future books, feel free to contact me. Keep in mind that you may become a bad guy.

Super thanks to all the fans of Breeze. I couldn't do this without you.

Acknowledgements

Cover photo by **Ed Robinson**

Cover design by https://ebooklaunch.com/

Interior design by https://ebooklaunch.com/

Proofreaders: **Laura Spink, Jeanene Olson**

Final edit: **John Corbin**